QUEERSPEC

A Queer Speculative Fiction Anthology in Support of Trans Rights - Volume One

K Petry, Harper-Hugo Darling, Emily Devereux, Erin Carter, Hannah Brown, O.E. Flynn, IJF Dymock, Riley Klay Ridgway

Altersphere Publishing

Book cover and interior design by Emily Devereux

1st edition 2026

CONTENTS

PREFACE

Near the end of 2025, the United Conservative Party of Alberta invoked the notwithstanding clause to shield three anti-transgender bills from court challenges, shielding these bills from being subject to the Canadian Charter of Rights and Freedoms. This anthology exists in resilience and defiance to the hostility and harm caused by this legislation.

Despite the notwithstanding clause, the battle against these laws continues. The royalties from this anthology are donated to the Skipping Stone Foundation's Trans Affirming Legal Fund to support these efforts.

A huge thank you to all the participating writers—it goes without saying, but the anthology would not exist without your contributions. The comradery and support from this group has buoyed my spirits. In addition, a special thank you to Colin Kiddinc, who provided editing notes for many of the stories.

Queer joy, queer rage, and queer resilience. Our stories cannot be erased.

To make an additional donation to the trans legal fund or learn more about Skipping Stone: https://www.skippingstone.ca/legalfund

To learn more about the continued legal battle: https://egale.ca/egale-in-action/fight-isnt-over/

For 2SLGBTQI+ resources and information: https://alberta.cmha.ca/lgbtq2s-resources/

Some stories in this anthology contain strong language and sensitive themes. Full content warnings can be found at the back of the book.

ABOUT THE STORIES

The Tale of the Necrobotanist by Kaitlyn Petry

Deep in the dark of the woods, villagers warn of a powerful, evil NECROBOTANIST. A what?? A necrobotanist! This is a tongue-in-cheek exploration of death and what's different led by a non-binary knight who isn't afraid to explore what's lurking in the darkness.

Communication specialist by day, pop-up bookstore owner also by day, mom to one kiddo and one cat, and busy speculative fiction writer—Kaitlyn always has something on the go and probably will not respond to your email in a timely manner.

Neptune Rising by Harper-Hugo Darling

A chaotic queer friend group filled with love and sacrifice is tested when a newcomer is introduced.

Balancing both fiction and nonfiction professionally since 2015, Harper-Hugo lives with their wife and three cats in Edmonton. Their heart belongs to horror, fiction, gory details, and queer as a verb.

Reforged by Emily Devereux

Gwen travels across the desert in hopes of learning how to use magic to reforge her body at the Sage's Spire. Will an unexpected meeting with the god of knowledge and healing destroy her, or give her everything she's ever wanted? A Crossworld universe story.

Emily is a nerd of many stripes and lives a life full of roleplaying games, reading, and chemistry.

More about her young adult fantasy series, Crossworld: Ascension, can be found at: https://emilydevereuxbooks.com/

The Thirsty Armadillo by Hannah Brown

Set in a Western fantasy world, a cowboy and an armadillo archaeologist (wearing a cowboy hat) save a team of expert dino diggers in iconic Drumheller, Alberta, by finding a mystical peppercorn that has miraculous healing properties.

Hannah Brown is a queer writer exploring fantasy and science fiction after publishing exclusively poetry and nonfiction. She is very excited about this first step in embarking upon the journey of fiction for this anthology, which upholds values dear to her heart. Through her work, she hopes to help those who feel weird and misunderstood laugh a little about their troubles, and let them know that they are not alone.

Tunnel by Erin Carter

Teenagers! In Edmonton! Fighting Monsters!

Erin Carter is a queer library worker living on Treaty 6, Métis Region 4. She likes to write about spiders.

Five Clouds, a Little to the Left by O.E. Flynn

A chilly November morning in 1983 takes a turn with the sudden appearance of an old flame. However, that's not the only turn history will take today.

O.E. Flynn is an author living in the beautiful city of Torrington, Alberta. A beautiful queer woman with a luxurious coat, she learned to read thanks to the PA system in the local museum and is certainly in no way a haunted, taxidermized prairie rodent.

Rite of Passage by I J F Dymock

When faced with the stern judgement of a hero you look up to, you balk from expectations and judgements of who you were to help shape yourself into who you are.

Born into decades of interesting times, Isaac found succor amongst the fantastic winds of words and fiction. Writing is his passion and hopefully his career, eventually. A romantic spirit that loves exploring worlds unseen by modern eyes until they are shared on a written page.

Find more of their work at: https://libraryunderthestairs.wordpress.com/

Welcome to HEL by Riley Klay Ridgway

The year is 2091. After a tumultuous 2020s, Alberta has become its own country, Free and Independent Democracy of Alberta (FIDA). Suffering from ever-growing wildfires, hailstorms and economic struggles, the people of FIDA elect a NeoTrumpist party that ships their scapegoats to outer space. This story documents a group of queer folks who are forced to build a new life on a distant planet.

Riley Klay Ridgway is an author and artist living on Treaty 7 territory. Through their writing, they explore inter-personal relationships and identity. In their artistic expression, they hope to remind others that while the journey may feel lonely, we are not alone.

THE TALE OF THE NECROBOTANIST

BY K PETRY

There are long and winding trails through the dark forest. Undergrowth cut back, trees removed, dangers abated. This is not one of those trails.

The locals pointed it out—*take the western path, the one behind the apothecary. You'll pass a tree cleaved in twain, a still pond, a fox den.* Jaime finds it only because it's marked. Scuffs in the grass, a sign nailed to a tree: "Do not enter."

The trees barely part here, the barest hint of an old path thick with new growth. The closeness of the brambles doesn't deter Jaime. They're an adventurer, after all. Wading through the dense thicket, their sword hews branches and twisted limbs with ease, leather bracers deflecting the skeletal trees clawing for fabric and hair.

Moving further into deepening darkness, Jaime reflects on the circumstances that brought them first to the village and then to this trail.

A series of disturbing tales barely overheard at the neighbouring tavern. Snippets caught over the drinking of wizards, the snapping of fighters, the laughter of bards, and the brooding of rogues. Sitting alone in the busy tavern, nursing an ale as amber-brown as their eyes, Jaime had listened and observed, well accustomed to picking up jobs by piecing together others' stories. One can't wait around for a local to ask for help or approach a guild to see what's posted—not when they're considered "a little bit odd."

So, they listened. According to talk, a handful of ill-fated companions had failed to return from a once-sleepy village. Despite an interest in gossiping, none of the other adventurers seemed keen to go looking for those missing.

But Jaime was plenty keen. Keen to be away from the crowded taverns, the choked roads, the busy paths. Keen to be away from the quest givers and the innkeepers, tavern loiterers, and inquisitive locals. It was too loud, too busy, and expectations were looming over everything. Expectations on how to dress. How to act. What to say. You must curtsey, darling. You must sit with your ankles crossed, like so. You must never wear anything too comfortable, *or* too revealing. You must look at a man one way, and not another. Not like an equal, never that. You must keep your hands soft. Your fingers slender for needlework. Your chin tilted down. Take up only approved hobbies. Growing flowers. Painting pictures. Reading books.

Jaime only liked books about knights. Only liked growing flowers with thorns.

When you're a loner, you must be willing to do what others will not. So, Jaime set upon the road to the village with no companions to wrangle and no opinions but their own looming overhead.

They arrived in the village to the sight and smell of picked-over bodies in the streets. Homes were crudely barricaded with boards scavenged from the carts that would have taken goods to market, stalls that would have stood in the village square, and fences that would have kept the wolves at bay. Eerily quiet, it smelled like burnt and rotting flesh. A strange scent beneath that—a loamy, earthy smell. One of freshly-turned dirt in the garden. Damp, crushed grass and morning petrichor.

Several villagers were congregated within an old stone temple grown over with vines and moss, stones cracked with nature's attempt at reclamation. There, the tavern whispers were confirmed. Each night, the town was overrun with shambling skeletons held together by vines. Skeletons that moved with ease, as though their musculature was still intact.

Regrown.

The villagers had a tale to tell—a terrible power lived in the woods. A warlock. A powerful necrobotanist.

A what?

A necrobotanist.

Intrigued, if incredulous, Jaime accepted the directions. *Take the western path, the one behind the apothecary, you'll pass a tree cleaved in twain, a still pond, a fox den.*

Plunging through the undergrowth, they come upon the tree first. Struck by lightning, by the looks of the charcoal striations.

The pond next. The ground dips below the path and softly cups a pool of still rainwater like a hand raised to a mouth, ready to drink.

The fox den is dug from the rotting corpse of a fallen tree. Jaime waits quietly, but there are no sounds from within. Further down the trail, it becomes apparent what happened to the fox. As broken as the tree, its parts now a home for wriggling maggots.

Having run out of instructions and unsure of where to go next, Jaime listens to the woods. The air below the canopy is still and heavy, weighed down by condensation. Beneath the stillness, there are bird sounds, faint and far. Beyond that, the sound of rustling leaves, snapping twigs, softly churning undergrowth—worms and centipedes crawling through the dirt and the dry fallen leaves, spiders spinning their webs.

A loud snap. A shift. A breaking open of the earth.

Jaime clutches the hilt of their blade and moves toward the sound. Noises have never frightened them. Things that made others nervous—darkness, loneliness, differences—are all familiar.

They break through the brush into a clearing. The canopy is intact above, but the trees seem to have bowed around this patch of earth, enfolding it in a circle and hiding it from the path. Protecting it. A quick scan of the clearing paints a small rise of ground upon which a cairn of stacked, white stones marks what can only be a grave. A dense hedge of thorny brambles circles the rise, and across the path, a fallen tree is splayed, its rotting contents open to the sky, a patch of strangely mottled growths freckling its craggy surface.

The clearing is washed in the colour of a rosy sunset. Pink that breaks through clouds and canopy to dapple the cool, dark shade. The shade deepens to impenetrable darkness at the other end of the clearing. Something snaps behind them. Jaime turns and finds the forest they've just traversed as dark and foreboding as the woods on the other side of the cairn, night having reclaimed it while they hesitated on the edge of dread.

They step backward two paces into the pink light of the clearing and stop. Sticks snap. Leaves and brush rustle. Just a moment ago, the forest was still enough they could hear the spiders in their webs, but out of nowhere, a cacophony of sound erupts. Creaking, groaning, breaking and slithering. Jaime takes another backward step, sword raised, and their foot crunches something, a firm texture that gives way beneath the pressure. Their booted foot sinks into the rotted tree, and as it does, it crushes several of the strangely mottled mushrooms, releasing a gaseous odour that makes them cough.

Reflexively, they open their mouth and suck in more of the fetid air, breathing in the sour-smelling swamp. Lungs revolting, they cough harder until doubled over. The twig snapping pauses for a moment, then begins again, closer. When Jaime pulls their arm back from across their mouth, there are splotches of red on the brown sleeve.

Jaime staggers further into the clearing, unsure of where to go, where might be safe to fall to their knees while struggling for air. Their failing vision lands on the rise of dirt and the stone cairn upon it—just as it moves.

Swollen, heavy eyelids part. Above, a dark, starry sky is blotted in irregular shapes by the shifting tree canopy. At first, it seems like the sky is moving, like a child's spinning top. But the sky isn't the one moving.

With this realization, Jaime becomes aware of sensations. The ground moving beneath their back, soft and moss-covered, dampening their clothes. The occasional twig grabbing and scratching at their arms, whipping across the exposed skin at the nape of their neck. Something is wrapped under Jaime's arms, some kind of rope dragging them across the clearing. Jaime bucks and squirms, but they're weak. Already spent. It feels like a blacksmith is trying to hammer out a dent in their chest piece. Their lungs fill in short huffs and expel in time with the rapidly increasing thrum of their heartbeat.

Struggling weakly at the end of the tether, Jaime unceremoniously drops. The rope, which is not a rope, starts to unravel—vines. Long, leafy tendrils that untwist themselves as they recede. Jaime thrashes against them, finally breaking free enough to push into a sitting position and scrabble a few feet across the mossy, damp earth before taking full stock of their surroundings.

It's fully dark in the clearing now. The cairn and the small hill are directly in front of where they've been deposited, dragged around the perimeter of the bramble hedge. A sliver of moonlight gleams against the rounded shapes of the mound, casting it in a pale blue glow. Jaime squints into the dim light, suddenly able to make out darker shapes in the white. Eye sockets. The upside-down leaf of a hollow nose. The cairn isn't rocks, it's skulls. That's when they notice a glint of moonlight off burnished silver armour.

Letting out a strangled cough, Jaime takes in the bodies of the missing adventurers caught against the side of the thorny hedge. Dead, empty eyes look out of rotting faces, thorny red vines snake out of noses and mouths.

"Why did you come here?"

Jaime whirls toward the voice, but there's no one there. Just the small rise of earth and the grisly cairn.

"To... help the villagers."

"To help the villagers," scoffs the voice, mocking.

There's a long pause, then laughter seems to fill the clearing from every direction. Jaime's head swivels, just within the tree line, dark shapes move, skeletal figures creak and shake as laughter rises from rotted bellies.

Jaime presses on, cutting through the sound. "The villagers sent me here in search of a powerful necrobotanist—"

"A necrobotanist!" The voice ratchets up, the laughs emboldened.

"The... skulls... and the vines... the creatures..." Jaime coughs and sputters, defensive.

"*Necrobotanist.* Ridiculous."

"Then what are you?" Jaime asks.

"I *was* a druid." The skull at the top of the cairn swivels slowly until its empty eye sockets come to regard the adventurer below. "I once made my home in these woods. I traded with the village. I called myself one of them for a time."

"And ... now?"

"Now I'm dead." If a voice could contain a shrug or a look of derision, this one would. "Obviously."

Jaime's planned retort dissolves into furious coughing. They struggle to their hands and knees.

"Soon, you'll join me," the voice adds softly.

Standing, swaying, Jaime wipes their mouth on the back of a dirty sleeve, beginning to unbuckle heavy armour. The iron drops to the mossy earth with a clang, and they suck in a satisfying breath laced with rot and decay. Stepping away from the cairn, they search for a trail in the muck.

"Stay!" the voice surges forward, echoing around the edge of the clearing. "Stay for a while longer." And more softly, "At least until the end."

"I would rather die in the den with the fox." The adventurer spits red.

"Please?" the voice asks.

Jaime turns back, regarding the cairn with eyes like dark honey. "Why?"

"You were the first one... who didn't say they'd come to kill me."

The adventurer shrugs, wiping their mouth again, ignoring the red on their sleeve. "Doesn't mean I won't, or can't."

"Is there no alternative?"

"I don't know." Jaime shrugs. "Talk?"

"Fine," the hollow voice says. "Let's talk."

Jaime glances toward the woods, avoiding the sight of the bramble hedge with its grisly fortification. There's no home for them beyond the darkness. No one they'd like to see before they go. No voice they'd like to hear before they die. No warm bed they'd like to lay in before they rot.

Shrugging, they climb the rise of dirt towards the cairn. The stones at the base can be distinguished this close, a small foundation beneath the stack of three bleached skulls. There's no inscription, no adornments. Next to it, Jaime finds a spot to settle where it's relatively dry, the moss soft and comfortable.

"So why all this?" they cough, motioning around the clearing.

"Why not?" the voice asks flippantly.

"Do you need lifeblood to sustain your magics? Do you crave destruction to sate your vengeance?"

"Vengeance?" the voice barks, then softens. "No, not vengeance."

"Then why?"

"I said I used to live among the villagers," the voice continues as Jaime softens into the ground, body slackening as they recline. "I was... different. Strange to them. I was an outsider."

Brown eyes reflect the dark sky, memories there, in the shape of the clouds that pass before the stars. A child who sits alone. Who belongs nowhere. Not in their home with their family, not in the clothes they are forced to wear, not even in their own body.

"Is that why you left?" Jaime whispers.

"I came to live in the forest for a time."

"But?"

"They pursued me. The villagers. Constantly tormenting me. The children would throw rocks through my windows, the adults would knock over my cart and murder my chickens. They would dig up my plants and trample my garden."

"That's awful," Jaime murmurs, thinking of the child in the memories, knocked to the ground, dirt ground into their palms until they bled.

"People are awful," says the voice, thoughtful, as though regarding them.

"So when you died, you became the...necrobotanist? To exact vengeance?"

"No. When I died, the villagers dug up my grave and separated my bones. Trapping me here."

"And then the vengeance?"

"NOT YET!" The voice shakes the clearing, stones skittering away from the base of the cairn.

"Go on then," Jaime prompts weakly.

"I communed with the forest for many years," continues the necrobotanist. "Beyond my influence, the village grew and dwindled and grew again. Through my friend the fox, I watched from afar. Through my friend the hawk, I looked on. But the villagers trained the hawk. Killed the fox. I was completely, utterly alone."

"How long?" Jaime asks.

"Ten years? Or a hundred."

"Then why all this, why now?" They indicate the skeletal figures surrounding the clearing, the bones and the bodies and the rot.

The voice does not respond. In the silence, Jaime looks up at the small window of the night sky visible through the canopy, now beginning to lighten due east, still glinting with stars. Pin-pricks in the curtain of the dark. They press their fingers into the loamy, soft earth. Their heart is beating slower now, and their shallow, small breaths are slower too. There's a glimmer at the edge of their vision, and Jaime turns their head slightly. A tall, shimmering figure stands beside them. Light blue, the colour of the skull in the moonlight. The slender figure is clad in cropped trousers and a tunic lashed at the waist, long braided hair swept over their shoulder to reveal the high bones of their face, sharp like cut glass.

"You..." Jaime's words hitch with their breath. "Were lonely?"

The figure nods. The canopy overhead shifts, blocking the moonbeams and casting the clearing into deeper darkness. The voice, when it speaks, comes from every direction. "The world spins, and I am frozen to this spot. I can't move my feet, and my arms reach only a small circle around me. I try to reach for the world, but there's nothing to grasp. Around me, it's changing too quickly. The ground is eroding, and I can never find purchase. I pull grass out of the earth, dig into the dirt. When there's nothing else to hold, I dig into my own flesh. With the pain comes numbness. For a time, I feel nothing. I want nothing. I am nothing. And that is worse than wanting the world."

Jaime watches the sky turn above them, their eyes fluttering closed as nausea rises with the spinning of their vision.

"The forest wants to help me," the necrobotanist continues. "It grows closer, slowly. It reaches out its branches, boughs, and vines until I have something to hold."

Vines snake around Jaime's arms, anchoring them to the earth and pulling them down against the loam.

"The world slows its spin. I am aware of time again. I am aware of my emptiness. My unimportance. The world has abandoned me. Moved on without me. Forgotten me. At first, I want nothing to do with it. I remember moments of happiness, and the longing betrays me. Soon, I am nothing but grief. The anguish of being just as alone now as I was when I was a living thing."

Taking slow breaths, Jaime is quiet for long enough to notice the rotation of the night sky. The circling of the stars is like a pod of sharks around a speck of blood. The vines tighten, pulling at them slowly, so they hardly notice themselves becoming one with the brambles and the moss. "I have also been alone," they say. "For a very long time."

A breeze moves through the canopy, and the trees bend away from the clearing, opening up the view of the sky to reveal the full breadth of the stars above, so many, they are vastly beyond count. Not a pod of sharks, but a whole, boundless ocean. A salty tear traverses the short band of flesh from Jaime's eye toward their ear and collects along the highest bone of their cheek before soaking into the earth. The vines shiver with hesitation and, after a long moment, begin to retract.

"Here," the necrobotanist urges. "Look."

Jaime's head turns, watching as a small green plant struggles from the dirt. It pushes through the closely woven grass and thick moss until they take pity. Rolling onto one side and shaking the vines free, they gently help the little plant emerge. Once it's grown a few fingers tall, the plant blossoms into a delicate purple flower.

"Eat," the voice says. "And I'll tell you how to save the village."

Jaime regards the flower for only a moment before doing as they're bidden, plucking it and biting it from the stem. It grinds between their teeth, releasing a sweet, grassy taste that soothes their aching throat and flavours each deepening breath. They plant their hands in the moss and sit up, shifting to their knees and then to their feet. When no more vines are sent to ensnare them, no skeletons appear in the murky shadows, their eyebrows knit together in confusion.

"You're free to go," says the voice.

"The village?" Jaime asks, cradling their ribs with one arm while the other hand hovers by their empty scabbard.

"I do not need it," the voice says before Jaime can turn away, "as long as you return—willingly."

Jaime regards the cairn. Its stack of bleached skulls and nondescript stones now glowing faintly with the first red light of dawn. Trapped here, like its occupant, amid the circle of brambles and the bones of the many who had come to strike it down and failed. *Not all problems can be vanquished with a sword*, they think. *Not all different things are the monsters they appear to be.*

They consider a moment, and nod, before turning back to the still, dark woods of the empty forest.

Later, in the tavern, Jaime tells their story. And around them, a crowd gathers to listen. *There are long, winding tales about bright, sun-dappled forests. Undergrowth cut back, trees removed, dangers abated.*

This is not one of those tales.

Neptune Rising

By Harper-Hugo Darling

There was a large hare outside of Neptune's apartment building. Upon seeing Neptune, the hare stood on its hind legs, stretching up a paw, not in greeting, but in some sort of acknowledgement. Standing on its back paws, it was not hunched in the comfortable way hares sometimes did. It was twisted up, moving in a way that its body was visibly rebelling.

A blessing. Neptune lifted their chin and took in a breath of the breeze. It was the end of winter, but not yet the beginning of spring, that balancing act that Edmonton toddled on for weeks and weeks before eventually falling into Neptune's favourite season. They were not wearing a coat; they had grown up in Canada, and their pink lace camisole only made the chill more enjoyable.

Walking up to the glass door, they saw the same old notices taped down in the wind, next to three stickers that had far more staying power. They indicating no smoking, a rainbow flag, and a Boardstreet logo. Neptune wanted to use their keys to dig under the rainbow sticker and carve it off the glass, leaving a large sticky mark where it used to be. But there were cameras facing the entrance. Instead, they used their keys for their intended purpose and unlocked the first door.

Even after living there for four years, Neptune always got winded walking up the three floors. The white paint of the railing was fracturing away to reveal dark stained wood. Neptune dragged a long shimmering pink nail against the gaps, expanding them as they went. When they had made it to their floor, the underside of their nail had tiny chips of paint that they used their thumb to clean off. Neptune walked to their door and unlocked it, already hearing the voices of their friends beyond. A grin tilted up their glossed lips as they opened the door, and they heard three voices chorusing their name. Their smile was not a complete thing, and the chorus was discordant. One tone was missing, but they had expected that. They had known that. Pulling back their shoulders and locking the door behind them they kicked off their shoes before hurrying to the living room. A deep green velvet sofa was entirely occupied, and their large white cat, Whitman, was sitting on a hard plastic kitchen chair, looking very displeased that he had been too slow to claim a spot in the pile of people that occupied the obviously softer choice.

Bram, Min-seo, and Ever had made themselves more than at home in Neptune's absence, and each had a different mug sitting on the coffee table in front of them as they greeted Neptune with smiles. Bram was curled in on himself. On the left end of the couch, he was the closest to Whitman and that was likely by design. Min-seo was in the middle, wearing khaki shorts in the cool weather. A woman after Neptune's heart as always, though she was wearing a knit sweater with a heart pattern on the collar. Ever was closest to Neptune, and he got up as soon as he saw them, walking to the kitchen and pulling a beer out of the fridge for them. Taking the cool glass bottle, Neptune indicated for Min-seo and Bram to make room for them, and they did so, Min-seo leaning half onto Ever's lap, and Bram wrapping an arm around Neptune's shoulders leaning his head to press it against them with an exhalation of breath.

"I saw a hare outside. It was starting to get brown patches." Tilting their head to the side, Neptune forced a smile onto their face. "A good omen for Chleo's date?"

Bram shrugged. "Or a good omen for you and your ceremony. Spring is coming."

"Spring is technically here," Ever corrected.

"There is still snow on the ground." Bram shook his head.

"But it was plus twelve most of today," Ever argued back, a wolfish grin on his lips. It was there not for any specific reason outside of the fact that he was just a person who looked a little more like a wolf than most. At least he did when he smiled. Or frowned. Or glared. When he was neutral, he looked a bit more like a threatening husky.

Bram rolled his eyes at Ever, fiddling with a large black-stoned silver ring on his pointer finger. "It's not spring until I see the first fledgling magpie fluffing about."

"I agree with Bram," Min-seo told the two definitively, and Ever huffed back into the couch.

Neptune took a sip from their beer and didn't comment on the debate, mostly because they didn't know who they agreed with. In their opinion it could be spring and winter at the same time for all they cared. They were turning two subjects in their mind. Chleo's date. And omens.

Spring was change, spring was movement, spring was the end to winter stagnation. All of which boded well for Chleo. The woman had waited for longer than anyone could have expected her to. She had turned down opportunities and reframed her perspective over and over. Still, Neptune felt an itching under their skin. They didn't like that she wasn't here with them. They didn't like distance at the best of times. It felt cold in all the ways they hated.

All five of them lived in the same apartment building, the largest distance between them being Neptune on the third-floor centre-right apartment, and Chleo on the first floor farthest to the left. This was not an insurmountable distance, and as the designated cook, Chleo usually either cooked in Neptune's kitchen or brought baked goods up. Hours passed without her arriving, and Neptune was trying to understand how exactly the stove functioned. They were sure, once they got past that hurdle, they were capable of scrambling eggs. They had watched Chleo do it a number of times. But they had yet to clear that first jump.

Bram had arrived first and was standing on the balcony, spreading out cat food on the concrete. Whitman was loudly protesting this indignity from the window of Neptune's bedroom. He was never allowed out when Bram was feeding the magpies. Already some of the white, black, and blue birds were starting to arrive, landing on the black wrought iron, making quite a ruckus with their entrance and expectations. These were all older magpies; no younger ones with their feathers fluffed about with moulting had begun arriving yet, and privately Neptune admitted that it wouldn't quite feel like spring until they did.

Having put out a decent portion of food for them, Bram ran a hand through his red hair and surveyed the group, all waiting for him to leave. They still didn't trust Bram quite enough to eat this close to him, but one of the larger ones was looking like he might try diving in and out if Bram didn't get out of the way soon. So Bram nodded to the group, and went back inside, closing the sliding glass door behind him and pulling up a chair to the kitchen table, angling it so he would have a clear view of the squabbling birds.

Bram might have been the most beautiful human Neptune had seen. In mornings like this, it was more obvious than usual. His hair was dyed the red of strawberries, and his chest bound the flat of sea stones. His white button-up shirt was open with the warmth of the early morning. Neptune remembered days when he would wear sweaters under the sweltering sun. All of the progress, all of the change, curled back in on itself with a simple knock at the door.

Of Neptune's four friends, all had keys. None knocked.

Neptune looked at Bram, and without a word he began buttoning up his shirt, passing by them with a gentle hand on their elbow as he walked through the small kitchen to the door. First, he stood on his tiptoes to look through the peephole and frowned at whatever he saw. He looked over his shoulder at Neptune, who wrapped their own fluffy black robe closer around themselves. Under it, they were wearing bike shorts and a crop top. At the warned intrusion, all they wanted was to hide behind Bram like a scared child. But they lifted their chin and went to the door, twisting the lock and holding the metal doorknob for five seconds before pulling the door open.

Neptune's eyes went to Chleo, drawn like a cat to sunlight, the woman was on a spectrum of beauty that was altogether different than Bram. Not a difference in quality, but simply an incomparability. This morning her short brown hair was held back by a headband, which made the back of her hair stick out in spikes. Moles all over her tanned skin, there was a smile on her pale lips.

Next to her was a tall man, and a being completely out of Neptune's world. He was smiling at her. His thin lips pressed against short teeth, as he held forward a platter of what was surely Chleo's work. Sliced fresh bread from the bread machine she had bought for ten dollars at the thrift shop, cheese cut up, and small jars of jam collected from the farmers' market on High Street.

"The boy!" Neptune greeted, pointing at the man in front of them, and his smile slipped a little as he looked to Chleo.

Chleo gave a sheepish smile. "I hadn't told them your name," she explained to him.

"Well, then yes, it's me, the boy!" The man widened his smile. "Pierce."

"Pierce." Neptune nodded.

Ever had always been a man for timing, and as he came up behind the two standing in the hall, he wrapped an arm around Chleo's shoulder, leaning down to kiss her cheek loudly and reaching over Pierce to grab a slice of cheese. Pierce looked at the other man, blinking quickly as if he was not seeing properly. To be entirely fair, Ever was a man who earned second glances.

Despite his size, Ever was able to slip past Chleo and got through the door, reminding Neptune that they were currently standing in the way of the two others from getting into the apartment. Stepping back, they tightened the tie holding their robe closed.

"So, Chleo, I assume Pierce's presence means the date went well," Neptune began, looking over their shoulder at the two.

Bram was following Neptune, and they could see on his face a hesitation, one that they felt and were trying to squash within their own chest.

"Yes, it went really well," Chleo grinned, and the discomfort eased ever so slightly.

"Very, very well," Pierce confirmed, smiling at Chleo, and Neptune nodded, going to shuffle scattered papers off of their cherry-stained wooden table.

"Well, it is lovely to meet you then." Neptune moved away, going to put their handful of papers onto their coffee table. Coming back to the dining area between the living room and kitchen, they caught themselves avoiding looking at Pierce and tried to correct themselves, taking a long overview of the man.

He was tall, not as tall as Ever, and slimmer than the other man as well. He was also visibly, palpably, heterosexual and cisgender. Neptune could not have said how they knew this without resorting to stereotypes and vague hand gestures, but they did know it. It was not suspicion or anything lighter than certainty.

"It was so nice when I heard Chleo had friends in the building, I cannot tell you how many people I've met never talk to their neighbours." Pierce's teeth were clean, with a recently minted waft coming from his mouth, which meant he had to have brought a toothbrush. Expecting to stay at Chleo's. Or he borrowed hers. Both possibilities repelled Neptune.

"Yeah, no, we are so lucky that we have been able to live close," Neptune agreed because it was an easy thing to agree to. Because there was no reason not to agree.

"Where is Min-seo?" Ever asked. He had already sat on the couch, knowing that there wouldn't be space for all of them at the table and self-selecting the most comfortable spot that would be least likely to hurt his back.

"She's coming, I think," Bram answered, rubbing the back of his neck with his hand, looking quite jealous of Ever's distance from the four in the kitchen. Sidling up to Neptune, he put a hand on their elbow again, and Neptune tried to relax their shoulders.

"You have quite a congregation there." Pierce pointed out the window, and the second Neptune turned to look at the birds they knew would be waiting, they saw one looking back.

It seemed like a trick of the light at first, but as the magpie hopped closer to the window, Neptune was sure; instead of the black beady eyes they were used to having staring at them, they saw blue. The blue of stones at the beach. It was unnatural, and Neptune knew what it meant. An omen. A reminder, and they didn't want it.

"Yeah, we feed them," Neptune said to Pierce, turning away from the birds.

"You feed the magpies? A bit of a nuisance, aren't they?" Pierce questioned, frowning ever so slightly as Chleo pulled plates out of the cupboard.

"Depends on how you define nuisance," Ever chimed in from his spot on the couch. "If you define it as loud, boisterous, and aggressive then yes, but Neptune has a habit of enjoying those qualities."

"I wouldn't say it's a habit." Neptune let themselves smile a bit, pushing their black hair behind an ear.

"Magpies, Chleo, Ever, no, he is definitely right. You are a collector of nuisances," Bram grinned at Neptune.

"Chleo isn't loud, boisterous, or aggressive." Pierce's frown deepened, and Neptune looked to the blue-eyed bird outside the window.

"Give it time." Min-seo had entered soundlessly, but her arrival was not met with surprise by anyone but Pierce, who flinched at the realization that another person had entered the small kitchen.

He narrowed his eyes as he looked over the four people around him, calculations going on behind his eyes. "When Chleo said she had friends in the building, I didn't expect all of you to be friends with each other as well. Do you ever get noise complaints?"

Ever laughed loudly from the couch. "Did you happen to notice the neighbourhood you were entering? People mind their business here. The only time we got a complaint was when the landlord was showing off an apartment next to Neptune's."

Pierce crossed his arms over his chest.

"No, it's for the best." Ever waved away Pierce's visible discomfort as he got off the couch and went towards the table, grabbing one of the plates that Chleo had set down and filling it with food. "See, since all of us outside of Min-seo are white queers, they know we are too poor to afford better, but they leverage us to make the area seem more respectable to racists. So, it is really our civic duty to fuck around as much as possible without bothering our actual neighbours so our naturally gentrifying influence takes longer to ruin the neighbourhood."

This did not seem to impress Pierce, who was quiet as Ever slapped a piece of cheese on top of one side of bread and sandwiched it together with another slice of bread covered with strawberry jam. Ever seemed less inclined to go back to the couch though, and he leaned against the wall, watching Pierce as Chleo started making up her own plate.

Neptune frowned at the two men but didn't let their antagonism stop them from going to the table and getting their own slice of bread and putting a piece of white cheese on it without grabbing a plate.

Neptune had originally spent all their money buying a king-sized mattress, setting it directly on the floor with nothing left to buy a box spring or bed frame. It had been a surprise when Chleo gifted them a new in-the-box wooden bed frame. It was simple, stained leather-brown with an arch and wood bars that had come in very useful through the years. So laying in the bed, Bram, Ever, Min-seo, and Neptune were all hesitant to go too far in talking shit about Chleo.

The cherry-patterned bedspread tangled between them, and their window cracked open to let the cool snow-tinged air into their heady pile of naked bodies, Neptune was so close to contentment. They had been for a while. On the edge, so close, aching to fall over into total bliss, but just not quite able to fall over. Because Chleo wasn't happy.

As happy as Neptune was, it still itched under their skin that Chleo was on the other side of the building sleeping with a man who refused to eat out unless she shaved.

The details had dripped into their friend group slowly. It had started with small complaints mixed in like chocolate chips in cookie dough, but now they were sure to be on the receiving end of double chocolate brownies any time Chleo came over. It was a difficult balancing act between disapproval of Pierce's actions with support for Chleo's choices, and Neptune didn't know what would happen if they fell on one side or the other.

So, it was a release valve. The four of them in bed, having released their tension in one way, there was still something off, as invasive as a creeping thistle. A part of Neptune wanted to grab it by the stem and pull.

"I hate this Pierce character." Min-seo was the first to say something, and Neptune let out a loud breath.

"Me too!" they exclaimed, grabbing her hand and turning their head to look at her. "I don't know what, but something about him is setting me off."

"I thought I made it pretty obvious that I want the fight the fucker," Ever grumbled underneath Neptune and Min-seo's joined hands.

"You did," Bram confirmed from the other side of Neptune, running a finger over their hipbone.

Neptune turned to look at him, frowning. "What about you? I feel like you are better at judging people than I am."

Bram considered this for a long moment, the attention of all three of the other occupants of the bed on him. "I'm not better at judging people, I just trust my judgement more than you do. And I have been waiting for someone to say something, but yes, he skeeves me out too."

Neptune laughed and adjusted their newly dyed blue hair on the pillow. Theirs was the only black pillowcase on the pile of silk teal ones, and Ever was beginning to encroach on it, his hands on Neptune's chest.

"I can kill him," he told them, his voice low and smile sharp.

Neptune's laugh turned into a giggle as Min-seo used her grip on their hand to also pull closer. "I can help," she offered, sharp nails scraping against Neptune's skin.

"I can make it look like an accident afterwards," Bram put forward, his grin cutting in all the ways Ever's was sharp. Soon none of them were thinking of Pierce.

Fifty-three days of Chleo dating Pierce. In the times when a friendship is a chore, consistency is key. It is difficult at the best of times to maintain a relationship with someone who spends most of their time complaining. When those complaints are all about the same thing, and that thing is something the person refuses to fix, it scratches at the nerves.

Neptune didn't give up on friendships, though. They let changes come and go, and sometimes one friend needed more tending to. That was normal. It was the cause that got to them. The man himself. The one they had to see at regular enough intervals to be reminded of who he was, of the fact he was a full person, and of the fact that he didn't deserve all of the malice they held for him. As pleasant as he was in moments, he was also constantly corrosive. Eating away at the edges of every moment spent with Chleo. When he was there, and especially when he wasn't.

Still, Neptune held on like a terrier, locking their jaws around Chleo, around the moments when Chleo was herself, onto her throat, her lifeblood, her vital, queer, loyal, joyful, generous, kind moments. The flaws that shadowed Chleo in her best times were not enough to pull her away from them before, and they wouldn't be now. Neptune was determined. Even if they felt the rest flake away and forget why Chleo was necessary.

It could have been so easy to let her go. Neptune could feel Min-seo aching for it. Could feel Ever fighting his every instinct to cut her off.

And Bram was always there, his soft slow withdrawal away from Chleo. But Neptune was the strongest of them all, and they knew that, and their white-knuckled grip on the woman would not ease.

Going to a local coffee shop alone with Chleo was not unusual. Chleo worked remotely, and Neptune could sketch just about anywhere. The two had spent many hours with Neptune and their markers completely focused on one side, with Chleo and her open laptop and headphones blaring musical theatre. Today, Chleo wasn't wearing her headphones, but she also wasn't talking. It was not enough for Neptune to say anything, but it worried them.

It was hours into the hangout that Neptune first looked out the window. There was a tree swaying, a small thing, a baby compared to some of the oaks in the more residential neighbourhoods, with its branches twisting up rather than out. They had seen this tree and sketched it a number of times. It was not new to them, but there was something about the way it was shaking on that day. Its leaves didn't move in time with the thin trunk. Neptune looked back down at their sketchbook. They were drawing clouds from a dream, but there were no clouds in the sky. They were officially in summer now, and the sun shone through the large glass windows without impediment.

"Pierce asked if I wanted to move in with him." Chleo didn't look up from her laptop as she said it, but Neptune almost hurt their neck with how fast they snapped to stare at her.

A moment of silence passed. Neptune reached for their iced matcha latte and took a long sip. "Do you want to?"

"Well, it is in one of the new properties he is managing, so it would be an upgrade, and since we would be splitting rent I would be paying about as much as I do now for a better place, better neighbourhood." Neptune frowned at Chleo's words because they were not her own. A recited argument passed on from someone else. From Pierce.

"I thought you liked our neighbourhood," Neptune said quietly.

Chleo didn't respond, she just looked out the window at the tree, still shaking unnaturally.

The day of August 11th came, and Neptune wanted not to know what they knew. They also wanted Chleo to stop looking at them, knowing the same thing. Omens had come to them both, they both knew what it meant. Bram, Min-seo, and Ever hadn't mentioned seeing anything, and Neptune couldn't see the same knowledge in their eyes that they saw in Chleo's.

Before anything, Neptune wanted to believe in love. They wanted to believe that there was someone for everyone and multiple someones for certain people. More than that, they wanted it to be easier on their friend. They wanted their friend to feel the same love Neptune shared with Bram, Min-seo, and Ever. They were three times blessed with something that Chleo still had yet to experience and more than anything, they wanted to share it. Neptune could not pour more love into Chleo if the two had been lovers. Still, they understood craving.

Worse than craving though, was filling hunger with an unworthy substitute. Neptune believed that. They weren't sure if Chleo did. They wouldn't know before tonight.

It was evening when Ever returned from work, taking a shower in Neptune's bathroom before the four of them piled into his car. Chleo had her own car and promised to meet them there.

Only Chleo and Neptune knew what this ritual might bring, but there was something different in the air of the cramped car. Min-seo and Ever weren't bickering in the two front seats, they were simply holding hands. Bram was resting his head on Neptune's shoulder. Already, their skin was starting to cool, still, Bram kept close as if trying to warm them.

The parking lot they pulled into eventually was empty, the white lines stark against black asphalt. They looked almost freshly painted. As Bram clicked open the door for Neptune, they entered the warm night air. It was the beginning of August, and the night was a comfort in a way it had never been before. As their lovers gathered around them, they were tactile things. As if, for this moment, their love languages had aligned like planets and all were touch.

Neptune hadn't worn much, as they knew they would be going home with nothing. Their blue basketball shorts shimmered under the light from the lampposts. It was better lit than most parking lots at this hour and probably had cameras, but that wasn't going to matter. Any image of them that night wouldn't develop outside of a bright blue blur. Something that was faded and soft around the edges when they took selfies, almost able to be mistaken for a trick of the light, would encompass Neptune and everyone with them.

Ever was wearing fingerless gloves, and his skin was warm against their hip as he bumped closer to them. Min-seo was behind them, tying their long hair into a braid, and Bram was at their elbow, running his hand up and down, trying fruitlessly to bring heat to their skin. The air around them was beginning to fade into a blue haze, but it was still early enough that they were able to see. Able to connect with the part of them that wanted to lean into the touches and savour the contact with their loved ones. The part of them that felt their bare feet cool the pavement that still clung to the warmth from the sun.

It was then that they heard the second car. Pulling into the bright parking lot, Neptune looked through the windshield and saw two people, and knew what this night would bring.

Glowing, their footprints froze the neatly trimmed grass with each step, green blades becoming icicles and then cracking underneath them. It was almost the only noise in the empty night. As the group of five walked into the golf course, it was just the crunching of ice beneath Neptune's every step, and the struggling of Pierce in Ever and Chleo's grip.

His feet never touched the ground, and when they passed through a sprinkler, he was pelted with tiny icicles that had entered Neptune's orbit and spun out to cut against his skin.

They had been forced to drag him out of the car when he had first seen the beginning of the monstrous thing Neptune was becoming. Though his struggle was getting weaker, he would intermittently try to rip himself out of Ever and Chleo's grasp as Neptune grew in size and scope. Bram and Min-seo were trying to remain as close to Neptune as they could, holding onto each other's hands, and averting their eyes. It had been almost a decade, and still, they hadn't gotten used to it. So really, no one could expect better from Pierce. This was his first and would be his last time seeing a planet held in a person.

The rest were smart enough not to look, to follow Neptune's trail of ice and quiet crunching walk. Chleo was watching Pierce, the disgust on her face becoming clear. All the hesitation that had buzzed under her veins at the approach had been burned away by proximity and visual evidence that Neptune was a planet Pierce could never orbit. He had none of the grace, the care, or the love that it took for something so complicated and fierce. The ice didn't fill his veins with fear and glory, it simply made him shiver.

She had not needed to bring him. Neptune never would have said anything. Never would have pointed out the omens. But Chleo had felt the draw as certain as she now felt the need to step back, to walk slower, to let Neptune go further away to give a bigger radius of safety. It was an instinct Pierce would never understand, and now, she would never have to explain it to him.

As Neptune walked to the pond, stepping onto the water like a god, Ever and Chleo stopped. Chleo could see Min-seo holding Bram back from following his lover onto the frozen water. Min-seo pulled him by the hand and brought him to Ever and Chleo where they held Pierce.

Ever let Pierce's feet touch the frozen ground, and on instinct the man pulled himself away, trying to climb back away from the cold. Chleo's lip curled, and it was she that delivered the final hard shove. Pierce's knees cracked against the thick ice that had formed over the pond, and even when she tried to look away, Chleo was able to see the spider-like movements of Neptune darting close, and she felt the painful sting of the cold against her cheek as she turned away.

Looking away and up at the night sky, the light of the planet in front of them was filling the air like the aurora borealis, thick as pudding there in the centre. Chleo heard the crunching of ice and bone breaking between teeth.

REFORGED

BY EMILY DEVEREUX

Gwen was desperate not to let the desert break her, but she was dangerously close to dropping to her knees and allowing the sun to take her. Let her rot in the savage heat. Roast her body into a corpse.

But she couldn't. She knew she couldn't. For several fundamental reasons.

Firstly, and most immediately, her companions would not let her give up, nor could she let them down. Her friend Adriane, most of all. But to disappoint Master Kathan was also unthinkable. She'd worked hard the last four years for his approval, for her place in the academy—and for her spot on this very trek.

Their group of five—four students from the academy and Master Kathan leading the way—trudged on through the sand.

"Are we there yet?" asked Niko, the only Engineering student on this misadventure.

At this point, the question was nothing more than a humorless joke. There was some levity to the phrase the first day they spent in the desert, but on the second day, it had lost the thin veneer of wit.

They hoped to be out of the desert lands of Suraskrit and into the savanna of Oromu by the end of the day. It would have been more beneficial to travel under the cool moonlight. Gwen cursed each step she took under the blazing sun, feeling as if Kajiem, the fire god of this land, was bearing down on them with all her divine strength. Master Kathan forced them to march by daylight, fearing bandit attacks by night.

Gwen suspected the fear of bandits was nothing but a farce, and that traveling by daylight was an intentional obstacle set by the academy. Their instructors were not afraid of putting strain on their students to test their mettle.

"We'll make it," croaked Adriane, perhaps seeing the defeated look Gwen was sure was plastered across her own face.

Gwen only nodded, her throat too parched to brave her voice. It would come out too raspy, if it came out at all. A sip from her waterskin did little to quench her aching throat. She pulled her white hood further forward, blocking the unforgiving rays of sun from her face. Never had she felt a heat like this in her mountainside homeland.

They had brought a cohort of one student from each of the four branches of the academy—Medic, Defender, Historian, and Engineering. She was glad that only a single cohort of four had come, meaning she was the only Medic. The other students in her branch of the academy were not always kind. She was the only one in her year who had the rare gift of magical healing. In some ways she was celebrated for this immensely useful talent, however, the jealousy of the other students and the expectations pressed upon her weighed heavily.

"You wouldn't dare disgrace yourselves by *not* making it," Master Kathan's voice remained stern, despite its dry roughness. "You're lucky even to be on this journey."

A stark reminder, which Gwen did not require. The last year had been solely dedicated to staying high enough in the academy rankings that she would be permitted to travel outside of their home region of Celaigh for the fourth-year students' learning exchange.

She needed to go to Oromu, the land of Io, the god of knowledge and healing. To study books at the Sage's Spires, to train with master healers—to learn things she couldn't learn back home.

Things she urgently needed to know.

She was grateful that Adriane had managed to rank high enough to request being in the same exchange cohort. There were probably more interesting things that her friend, who was a Defender student, could have done for her training. Adriane was more focused on combat, being an archer and a mage attuned to Meyrin, the god of defence.

She was grateful to her friend for choosing to support her, rather than traveling to a master of archery or a Meyrin-attuned mage outside of the capital to train with. Adriane knew what was on the line for her. This could change everything for her.

That was the main reason she couldn't give up, despite the brutality of the sun. Not because of Adriane, or her academy instructors, or her duty as a healer.

It was for herself.

Master Kathan, at the head of the group, held out a hand, signaling them to stop. Gwen looked around for a sense of why he gave the direction, squinting to see the edges of the sand dunes around them better in the glaring light.

"What's wrong?" Talas, the Historian student, asked.

Kathan only put a finger to his lips.

Gwen braced herself as a gust of wind kicked up the sand around them, raising a hand to shield her eyes from the debris. She tried to listen, but heard nothing but the howl of the wind.

When the sand cleared, Gwen peeked over her robe's sleeve, blinking through the last of the settling dust. Something big and bright was hurtling toward them from the horizon. Gwen gasped and jumped back, though the ball of fire was careening toward Master Kathan.

Before the fireball could reach them, Adriane swept her hand outward and summoned a glimmering wall of magic in front of their group. The fire slammed into it, dissipating against the shield.

"Get down!" Kathan yelled, primarily to Niko and Talas, who had no magic and little ability to protect themselves against an onslaught of flame from a Kajiem-attuned mage.

Gwen crouched alongside them, her eyes flickering across the horizon, trying to get a handle on where their attacker was, and if there were more attackers. Adriane strung her bow without lowering her gaze, standing alongside Master Kathan in front of them.

Bandits. There really *were* bandits, though traveling by daylight had certainly not protected them.

Her heart threatened to hammer out of her chest. Only Master Kathan and Adriane were trained fighters. Gwen had some combat training, but had considerably more practice healing with her magic than hurting with it. The other two students would have had cursory combat training, like her, but nothing as intense as Adriane's schooling. The only weapons the non-Defender students carried were daggers.

Whoever had blasted the fireball at them had disappeared down the far side of a sand dune. Gwen turned to look behind them, and a shriek sputtered out of her throat. She hissed out a warning, "Behind!"

A group of three, almost blending into the sand in their loose, light-coloured clothing, was poised to attack. One stood back, aiming a bow, and the other two barreled toward them, the knives in their hands glinting in the sunlight upon their approach.

Adriane turned and let her arrow fly before the opposing archer could launch their own. Shimmering magic coiled around the arrow, propelling it faster and guiding its path. The bandit took the arrow to the neck and collapsed. Gwen didn't flinch from the flash of blood; she'd seen enough of it in her own training.

Gwen drew upon her magic, forming a ball of energy in her hand, then condensing it into a dart. She flung it at the faster of the two bandits charging at them, but the energy flew wide.

Gwen gritted her teeth and repeated the action. The bandit was drawing close, too close—but with a nearer target, she was rewarded with a strike to his shoulder.

But the bandit shrugged the hit off, continuing his charge—

Another arrow took out the bandit who was farther back, leaving only the one Gwen had injured, knives in both hands. His eyes were the only thing left uncovered by his sand-coloured wrappings, they were dark and hard. Ready to slash her open.

"Down!" Adriane yelled.

But Gwen froze in place, a shriek growing in her throat, her magic slipping through her fingers.

The bandit dropped to the ground before he could reach her.

An arrow pierced through his skull, the arrowhead pointing out from his right eye.

It took Gwen a moment to put it together. Since Gwen was blocking Adriane's shot, her friend had used her magic to loop an arrow around and strike him from behind.

Gwen let out a breath of relief, turning backward to her friend. "Thank y—"

What she saw behind her stole her words.

A blast of fire, bigger than the shield Adriane had summoned, washed over the magical defence and burned it away. Master Kathan stumbled back from the biting flames, losing his footing and falling backward into the sand.

Before the flames could clear, a volley of smaller fireballs raced through.

Gwen tried to turn away, but a fireball struck the side of her head. The searing pain was instant; the smell of her flesh was horrendous. She slumped into the sand and let the agony wash her consciousness away.

Sun. Fire. Sand.

Pain.

It was all Gwen could remember of the next days. Each time she woke, the agony rippled through her, and she let unconsciousness take her back. Drag her under.

She imagined her slumber as if it were the ocean. The cooling, rolling waves drew her underwater, into currents of healing.

In her dreams, she was separate from her physical form, her spirit watching her body rest on the ocean floor. Glimmers of sunlight washed over her face, now disfigured with angry, rippling red lines and puckered skin.

As if she could hate her body any more than she already did.

This journey was supposed to *fix* her body. Not make it worse.

All she wanted to do was to look at it and feel as if it were her.

She let her spirit drift through the currents, as far from her body as she could get.

A woman's voice pierced through the veil. "Kathan healed his face well, though there may be scarring without continued, intensive treatment."

"*Her* face." Adriane's correction was a careful, practiced balance between kind firmness and prickly annoyance.

"...Yes. Of course." The words were spoken in a dubious tone.

"Why hasn't she woken?"

There was a pause, wherein Gwen imagined the woman shrugging. "Your friend's body decided it needed rest, even with the help of your Master's magic. It still takes a lot of... her energy to heal."

Another pause.

"Dinner will be ready shortly," the woman said.

"I'm staying with her until she wakes."

The woman grunted softly.

Footsteps padded away. A door opened, then closed.

It didn't smell like home. Whatever place of healing they were in was full of unguents and healing herbs of a different variety than back in the mountains.

They were in Oromu, then. A whole different climate, and new herbs to learn.

That would have excited her, once.

The agony had subsided into a dull ache, stretching from behind her ear, across her cheek to her nose. Kathan had used his magic to speed her healing, but the burn had run deep. Such things still took time to mend.

Gwen was awake, properly awake, for the first time since the attack. Still, she was afraid to face consciousness. To open her eyes. To see her own face, not in her dreams.

With a deep breath, she opened her eyes.

Adriane was the first thing she saw, her friend's eyes full of concern. "Are you okay?" she murmured, taking Gwen's hand.

Gwen took several breaths before releasing her hand so that she could push herself up to a sitting position. Her muscles were stiff with disuse, and something dark and hopeless coiled in her stomach. "No," she answered. "How did you get me here? How long has it been?"

"With great difficulty." Adriane's brows furrowed. "It's been a week or so. We took turns carrying you until we were out of the desert, then we were able to get a horse once we got into Oromu."

She'd been unconscious for a week? A facial burn was serious, but not so serious that she should have been out for days. Especially with the help of Master Kathan's healing.

It felt as if something within her had unraveled. Then she'd sunk into despair.

"Where are we? Mirune?" Gwen's throat was scratchy, as if she was still half-dehydrated in the desert.

"Yes, we made it to the capital."

"Are the others...?"

"They're okay. Nothing Master Kathan couldn't fix quickly."

At least there was that. Gwen ran a hand through her hair, only to gasp at its length.

"It... your hair burned. I'm sorry. I tried to cut it to make it look alright with the other side."

"Can I see?" Gwen asked, her voice small.

A grimace passed over Adriane's face, which did not inspire confidence. Slowly, her friend stood, then fetched a hand mirror from atop a cabinet on the other side of the room. Gwen clutched the looking glass, and braced herself.

It was just like in her dreams. Puckered, red skin—half her face. It stopped shortly before her eye, sparing her sight. Half her hair was shorn short, as she'd had it as a child. As it wrapped around the back of her head, it became longer, Adriane having blended the lengths as well as she could as it transitioned to her longer, shoulder-length hair.

She always wished she could be beautiful. Never was, never could be. Especially now. With healing, the scars may fade over time, but with the intensity of the burn, she didn't know if it would ever be pristine skin gracing her face.

She didn't have it in her to cry. She could only let the mirror drop onto her lap and close her eyes. Pretend things were not like they were.

"Gwen." Adriane removed the mirror from her lap, then grasped her hands. Gwen dared to reopen her eyes, to meet the intense gaze of her friend. "You can still do what you came here for."

Gwen swallowed. "The woman who was here. Was that...?"

"Aliyah. Yes."

The healer they'd come all this way for her to learn from. "She doesn't know how to teach me what I need to know."

"You don't know that—"

"I do." Gwen released Adriane's hands and then pulled herself out of bed, though she was unsure where exactly she was going—she just needed to be *up.* It turned out that "up" was disorienting after being off her feet for so long, and she clasped onto Adriane's shoulder to steady her balance as her head spun. "She struggled to call me 'her'. Do you really think she knows the magic that can help me?"

Adriane bit her lip. "So what? She's one healer. There are others here, more people with healing magic than any other region—someone will know. Master Kathan said so."

So he had.

There was a book, heavily damaged, that Master Kathan had given her three years ago. It was a flamescribed text from Suraskrit, the horrid desert land she'd almost just died in. Like the other books owned by the master healer, the remaining pages described various medical treatments. The fire mage who had scribed the book had detailed careful illustrations of plants that could be used to aid in healing.

Healing. Or changing bodies in other ways.

Gwen had all but memorized the page her master had flipped to.

Fireclover.

A hardy plant that survived harsh conditions, whether hot or cold. It survived in the mountain climate back home in Celaigh, thankfully. Kathan had given tinctures of it to Gwen. Though she was fifteen now, her voice hadn't yet dropped, nor had she started to grow facial hair.

The effects of the plant had made it harder to tell that she was born in a way that did not indicate to others that she was female, though she knew in her heart what was true. And there were many others like her, who felt the same way she did. Enough that a herbalist had recorded the effects and usefulness of fireclover.

She'd told her parents first.

"My name is Gwen, and I'm a girl."

After she said it, she'd exhaled the breath that it felt like she had been holding her whole life.

It had taken everything. Everything in her to say those words. They'd come out of her mouth with confidence, her head held high, and then she slumped, her bravery spent.

Her parents had stared at her across the kitchen table, the smell of freshly baked bread permeating the room, and her memory of that day. The scent had always made her feel at home; though right then she was not so certain.

Her mother spoke first. "I don't understand."

"You don't have to understand." Gwen leaned back in her chair, crossing her arms, as if that would protect her feelings—armor her heart against anything her parents could say. "You just have to know."

And accept it, ideally.

They had. After some time.

The academy had taken it alright. They had to. With how rare healing magic was, they couldn't afford to lose her—their only healing mage in her year. But they'd converted a storage closet into a single-occupancy dorm for her, rather than moving her to the girls' dormitory.

Acceptance without acceptance. Tolerance without understanding.

It was alright. But it wasn't enough.

Her heart ached and ached, and when Master Kathan had told her the healers in Oromu might know more... there was a moment of relief. And then yearning. And then she put everything she had into getting here.

"Where are you going?"

Gwen hadn't consciously realized she was moving toward the door. She stopped. She didn't even know where they were—perhaps the healer Aliyah's house?

But she did know where she was going.

"The Spires," she whispered, almost reverently. "Are you coming?"

Adriane hesitated, surely wanting her to rest, to eat something, to take a moment to recover before diving back into her quest. But then she nodded. Because her best friend knew what she needed most.

Hope.

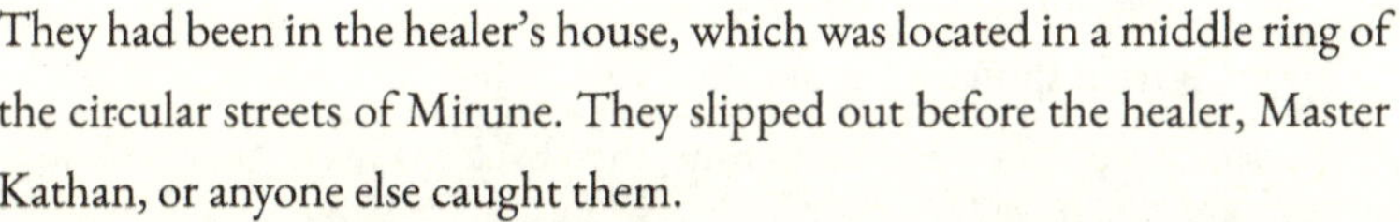

They had been in the healer's house, which was located in a middle ring of the circular streets of Mirune. They slipped out before the healer, Master Kathan, or anyone else caught them.

It was not difficult to find the Sage's Spires. It stood in the centre of the city, a sprawling complex with walkways stretching between sky-high towers of different colours. Though the academy's fortress was imposing, Gwen had no idea that architecture of such marvel was possible. Between the towers, gardens sprawled, each plant having a small placard indicating its name and native region.

Gwen gawked at it all, passing through the gardens hastily but not without appreciation. Adriane helped steer them to the middle of the grand complex—the tallest spire, whose ground level was an open-air atrium with large, arched entrances. The floor was a shining marble which Gwen nearly slipped on the moment she stepped on it.

At the core of the atrium was a spiraling staircase, leading up into the towers of knowledge. Gwen's heart leapt—she was *here,* finally, and with such a great store of books and scholars, surely there was something that could help her, even if the healer could not.

The two of them stopped short when a figure emerged from the other side of the staircase and blocked their path to the spiraling stairs. The only person who appeared to be in the atrium with them—a hunched woman in a tattered grey robe. The gnarled walking stick she bore tapped on the marble as she approached them, her long, straight white hair swaying with each purposeful step.

"Are we allowed to be here?" Gwen squeaked out, her heart in her throat.

The crone—or the sage, perhaps—looked her up and down. "You were expected to be here," she said, each word spoken with weight.

"What?"

"Come, come." The elderly sage turned to the staircase, beckoning her to follow. "You only. Not your friend."

"Wait!" Gwen spun to Adriane. "I... you..."

Adriane's eyes flickered to the crone, then back to Gwen. "I don't know that we can trust her."

Gwen took a steadying breath. "I think I have to. But leaving you behind—"

"She's come with you far enough," came the sage's voice. The woman had started ascending the stairs, turning back to them to speak.

The truth of it rang through Gwen's chest, though she didn't understand. *Who is this woman?* Something about her seemed... intense. Important. Gwen's skin prickled as she felt the aura of magic surrounding the woman.

Adriane's brows furrowed, but she gave Gwen a stiff nod. "Go. I'll be right here whenever you're done..."

A concoction of feelings melded within Gwen. Excitement. Fear. Confusion. But her heart pulled her toward the sage. She nodded back to her friend, then bounded after the crone.

They ascended the staircase without speaking, only the echoing taps of the sage's staff punctuating the silence. They kept rising past floor after floor, Gwen glimpsing rows of bookshelves, atria lined with statues and tapestries and illustrations, desks for scholars to study at.

Is anyone else here, in the tower? Gwen wondered. She recalled seeing some people strolling through the gardens outside, though she hadn't paid them much mind. Perhaps all the scholars were buried deeper in the towers, but it felt eerily empty and quiet having only seen the elderly sage inside.

Her legs ached, and she was panting by the time they reached the ultimate height of the tower. Gwen stepped off the staircase onto level ground, her knees wobbling. Perhaps she *should* have eaten something before coming here.

And yet, in the sage's presence, everything seemed to be as it should be. A strange sense of peace had washed over her.

Gwen stared at the high, vaulted ceilings as the crone led her through an arched doorway, down a hall lined with velvet carpeting, and then into a small, circular room, which was significantly more simple than the rest of the tower. The floor was stone, the wall was stone, there were no paintings or art or books—it was simply empty. No windows, and only the door that they had entered from.

Gwen shivered.

The sage summoned an orb of light before shutting the door behind them, sparing them from what otherwise would have been utter darkness.

"Why are we here?" Gwen asked, her voice wavering.

"Yes, that is the question, isn't it?" The sage cocked her head. "Tell me, Gwen, why did you come here?"

The back of her neck prickled. "H-how do you know my name?"

A faint smile stretched across the sage's wrinkled face. "I foresaw you coming, dear."

"You're a seer?" Attuned to Io, then, just like her. Though with a different subset of magical abilities that the god provided. Though insight powers were common among Io-attuned mages, true seers who could divine the future were rare. Gwen hadn't heard of there being any since the end of the war between the gods, a century ago.

The sage clasped both of her hands on the top of her staff. "You haven't put it together, child?"

Gwen shook her head slowly.

"I am Io."

The words took a moment to sink in. Gwen's first reaction was disbelief, but swiftly the pieces clicked into place. Not only was the sage a seer, she had an aura of power that was like nothing Gwen had felt before. She had never met Meyrin, the god of her own realm, though he occasionally visited the academy.

They *had an aura of power*, Gwen corrected herself mentally. Io aligned themselves with neither the masculine nor feminine.

A god who could, perhaps, understand her.

Or maybe not understand her at all.

"I know why you came here," Io continued. "But I need you to say it aloud."

"I came here..." Gwen paused. The fact that she was speaking with a *god* froze her in place, the immortal's aura overwhelming her.

Why would Io deign to speak with her, to foresee her coming here?

Gwen was just a random mortal—not even from Io's own region. There was nothing important about her, nothing that should interest a god.

Unless Io really did understand her, and why she had come here.

Her heart in her throat, Gwen dared to meet the god's gaze. "I came here so that you could fix me."

The god tilted their head, their eyes glinting with something akin to disappointment. "Fix you? I cannot do that, Gwen."

A bolt of pain flared through Gwen's chest. Had she finally attained hope, only for it to be crushed? *"Please."*

Io raised a hand, stopping Gwen in her tracks. "I cannot fix what is not broken."

"But I *am,*" Gwen bit out, surprised at the venom in her own words. Unsurprised at the tears biting at her eyes.

She was tired of trying not to hate herself.

She did not break eye contact with the god, staring into the cold, grey eyes of the sage. Bidding them to *please,* teach her what she came here to know. What she now knew the healer Aliyah could or would not teach her.

"Do you know why Kajiem created fireclover?" Io asked.

"No," Gwen said, thrown off by the sudden mention of the god of fire.

"Kajiem, in the early years of us gods walking these lands in mortal bodies, bonded with a man as her incarnate. It was a short-lived experiment. She hadn't realized her own preference for femininity until she walked the World in a body that did not suit her. It disturbed her greatly, in fact. She has only formed incarnate bonds with women since then. The gods all have a preference for the gender of their vessels... except for me. I am neutral about my form. None are good, or bad, they just *are.* Just as your body is."

Gwen clenched her teeth. "Are you saying I should be like you? That I should just... deal with my body, as it is?"

"Patience. I have not finished the story." Io took a breath, then continued. "When Kajiem realized that there were mortals that felt as she did when she walked in a man's body... that some were born into bodies that did not suit them, she created fireclover. While not a perfect solution, as you well know, it was what she could do to help them. To stop their bodies from shifting in uncomfortable ways, if nothing else."

Gwen listened intently. Indeed, fireclover had helped her, even if it had not changed her body in every way that she hoped.

Io shifted their weight, gripping their staff for balance. "I realize that not all are like me. Able to tolerate their bodies, whatever their form is. You want to change, as some do, and that is fine, Gwen.

"But I also want you to know that you are not broken. You are not something to *fix*. You are as much a woman in your current body as I am neither woman nor man in mine. There is beauty in who you are—and in whomever you'd like to become. And perhaps, in embracing who you are, you will help others, too. As Kajiem did."

Gwen wasn't sure what to make of that. That something good could come out of her own suffering.

She supposed that would depend on what happened next. "Can you teach me, then? To help myself, and others?"

"Yes."

Gwen's heart fluttered. "Why?" she couldn't help but ask. "Why me, why bother?"

"Because you deserve it. And because of everything that comes after."

A cryptic response. Gwen supposed she could expect nothing less from a god who could divine the paths of the future.

The crone's eyes flickered. "But it will hurt."

Gwen scoffed. "It doesn't matter." To hurt once, and have her body forever? Easy exchange.

"And we'll need fire."

Fire. After the desert, after the attack, flames were the last thing Gwen wanted. Flames had hurt her, burned away her face, her hair, her hope.

Destruction. That's what she'd thought fire was, and it felt against her very purpose of coming here—because she was tired of being pulled apart at the seams. She wanted to be whole. New. Restored. The opposite of her conception of flame.

Yet, she set aside her dread and allowed the fire mage that the god called upon to join them in the stone chamber.

She had faith. Not in the god, but in herself, and the choices that she made to get to where she now stood. She had come here for a reason, and she wasn't going to flee.

It was never, or now.

Between the divine sage and mortal mage of flame, they remade Gwen's body.

These flames were not to burn her. The flames were divine femininity, they were life, they were rebirth. They were something holy that Gwen could not put into words, something seared deep into her psyche until she knew, she *knew* that she could work her healing magic along with a fire mage to morph others the way they morphed her.

The god had not lied. The agony was so much worse than the bandit's fireball.

To her very core, she knew it was unfair that she had to endure this. But this was not a pain that Gwen could sleep through, nor did she want to. This was a pain with a purpose, with an end. A hurt she could bear despite its unjustness, knowing that she would emerge from it anew and with the knowledge she came for:

She was whole. She was perfect. Now, and before, she was everything she was meant to be.

In the divine flames, Gwen was reforged.

And she emerged ablaze.

The Thirsty Armadillo

By Hannah Brown

One lonesome day on the dusty trail, a bisexual cowboy by the name of Peppercorn Gary nearly steps on a three-banded armadillo curled up in a ball.

Withdrawing his foot, he takes inventory of his surroundings. The barren landscape is many shades of light brown, and hoodoos beckon in the distance. The horizon is wide and endless, and the sky is so large here that one can't help but ponder the meaning of infinite. Nearby, there is a scorpion poised to attack the armoured creature, but it seems to be struggling to find a point of entry. The scorpion throws its arms in the air, as if in defeat, and scuttles away before Gary even has time to consider how to prevent it from harming the armadillo.

"The scorpion is gone, friend. Figured you were more trouble than you were worth." Gary doesn't mention that the single type of scorpion that populates Drumheller, Alberta, is quite harmless to most humans. He wonders absently if that's true for a creature so much smaller than him, such as a three-banded armadillo.

The armadillo slowly unfurls. The process is fascinating to Gary, who marvels at the lengthening of the armoured sections of the creature's torso. Once he is fully extended, Gary notices that he is wearing a fashionable cowboy hat, roughly the same shade as his own, and incidentally, their surroundings. The main difference is that the armadillo's hat doesn't have an intricate, criss-crossing band of varying hues of peppercorns encircling his head.

He puzzles over this, not only because the armadillo is wearing a hat, but that there is a hat made for him that so perfectly complements his eyes, and what a species native to South America is doing so far north. Gary introduces himself, somewhat humbled by the creature's charisma. The creature projects a soft, deep male voice into his head.

"Pleased to meet you, stranger. My name is Paprika Sam." They tip their hats to one another. "Thank you for letting me know the scorpion was gone. Sometimes it feels like I curl up for hours, and I am never quite sure when it is safe to open up again. And I'm starting to get hungry."

Peppercorn Gary nods in understanding. He, too, has felt the need to hide from danger without knowing when it will pass. "What brings you to this barren landscape?"

The armadillo grimaces, insomuch as an armadillo can grimace. "I'm in search of a fresh water supply for my team. We have a dino dig site a few leagues from here, and find ourselves in a bit of a bind."

Peppercorn Gary frowns back at the armadillo. “I don’t mean to offend, but I wonder why they sent such a small member of their team. Are you the only armadillo on your team, or are you a team of armadillos?”

Paprika Sam blinks back at Peppercorn Gary, as if he were asking him why the sky is green. In a careful voice, he answers. “My team is made up of humans, of course.”

Gary is baffled by this answer, wondering if the armadillo, who seems to be aware of at least some of his unique abilities, knows he is a different species from his colleagues. Sam continues.

“But I suppose they sent me because I have a higher tolerance to dehydration. I can search longer and harder and spend more time in direct sunlight than any of the others, who are doing their best to stay out of the sun. And I can store water bags under my armour plates since mine are extra airy.” He waggles the equivalent of his brows, which is a line where his head armour meets the top of his eyes. The effect makes it so his entire head armour plate wiggles up and down several times. It is strangely hypnotic.

“I see,” replies Gary, somewhat dazed. “And what, may I ask, happened to your water supply?”

Sam looks at Gary speculatively, weighing his answer.

“In our field of work, we make enemies. Not everyone is willing to accept the evidence that our world is significantly older than their sensibilities suggest, or rather, their God. Suffice it to say that some creationists have taken it upon themselves to sabotage any efforts made to unearth dinosaur remains.”

The armadillo then sits down and proffers a sack from his midsection, which Gary didn’t notice earlier. He pulls a piece of fruit leather from the sack and munches on it philosophically.

“They took our water and our horses. Now, most of us are too dehydrated to be of much use.”

Gary frowns at this. He doesn't understand why the truth is so disturbing to some people. He doesn't have much time to ponder this, as the armadillo continues.

"And what is it that you are doing out here, fine sir?"

Gary ponders how to answer this question. He is in the possession of rare, precious knowledge that he wishes to hoard, yet he senses no ill will or greed from this mysterious character. He also recognizes that his quest, and that of the armadillo academic's, are very much in alignment. Reaching a decision, Gary replies.

"There is a rare type of peppercorn in these parts, and I intend to find the source."

The armadillo munches on the tough strip of fruit. "Peppercorns, eh?" he says out of the side of his mouth. "My, my. I thought they were restricted to black, white, pink, green, and Szechuan. But I assume there is more to it than that?"

Gary takes a deep breath, wondering if his ancestors would smile or frown upon his choice to trust another soul with their collective peppercorn secrets. But this one piece of information doesn't have to reveal the breadth of his great quest.

"My good man, there is more to peppercorns than you could imagine. I believe that our quests may lead us on the same path. You see, this peppercorn is said to relieve the life-threatening effects of dehydration by replenishing the cells in the body with water. Each one is the equivalent of a week's worth of hydration for any being, which is part of their magic, somehow without drowning or overwhelming the system."

The armadillo ponders this, still chewing on the same piece of fruit leather he's been working on for the last minute.

"If what you say is true, then we may indeed find it prudent to join forces, so to speak. At the very least, I could do with your assistance in spotting scorpions. And you, well, I suppose you don't need me at all, but I would be extremely grateful for your help, should you find yourself willing to aid a team of paleontologists in the arid lands of Drumheller."

Gary, who has a soft spot for dinosaurs and other long-gone ancient beings, finds himself very drawn to the idea of helping. He also wonders if the team might come across any fossils or other evidence of peppercorns, and what those findings might tell him about lost varieties and ancient lineages.

"I will help you," he says, "on the condition that should you find any evidence of peppercorn plants or their use, culinary or otherwise, in your academic career, past, present, or future, you share it with me, and only me. And that my discoveries, regardless of how miraculous they seem, remain a secret among your team."

Paprika Sam's face warms into a bemused sort of smile, perhaps wondering why this man is so fixated on peppercorns. "I will, of course, need to run it by you should such evidence prove to have larger implications than anything unique to the world of peppercorns. We have a responsibility to share useful knowledge with the wider public. These peppercorns we are about to find, for example, could help millions, even billions of beings suffering from water shortages."

"I understand, but please understand me," says Gary gravely. "If even a whisper of such knowledge gets out, there are people, dangerous people, who are looking for that information. You do not want to get involved with them. It's best to keep things quiet."

Puzzled, and somewhat concerned now, Sam replies. "If you think that we are safe even looking for these, then I will trust you." Gary nods in response.

Paprika Sam brandishes his paw to Gary to shake. They do, and the deal is set.

When Paprika Sam is finally finished with his fruit leather, the sun is nearing peak height.

"So, I have surmised that the peppercorns could be found in one of three locations. The nearest to us is a small cave carved into the side of a hoodoo shaped like a ram's horn, very distinctive."

Paprika Sam nods, his eyes bright with hope. "Lead on, my good man."

The walk is short and hot, as there isn't a cloud in the sky, and they find what they are looking for quickly and without fuss. The tall, pillar-like structures with their sandy colouring stand out against the clear blue sky. Concentric rings run the entire length of the columns, showing the effects of thousands of years of erosion on layers of rock of differing hardness.

The ram's horn hoodoo, with its strange, unnatural twists and turns, strikes a sense of wonder in them both. This unique formation surely merits further study from a certain armadillo academic when the time is right.

They proceed, getting close enough to the hoodoo to see that there is indeed a small cave carved in its surface. Unfortunately, it is rather high up, and there doesn't seem to be any easy access point.

Peppercorn Gary doesn't seem concerned in the slightest. He merely reaches for his backpack and pulls out a grappling hook, throws it to the mouth of the cave, then tugs on the rope to check that it is secure. Without another word, he begins the short climb to the cave entrance.

Once he reaches it, he shouts down to the armadillo.

"Just sit tight there, I won't be long," he says, and ducks his head inside.

The cave is cramped, not even tall enough for Gary to stand to his full height. He has to crouch awkwardly to get around, and hopes that he finds what he is looking for quickly. His quads, though very developed, may start to burn soon.

After a thorough search, he finds no evidence of peppercorns whatsoever. What he does find is a nest of black widow spiders. Remaining calm is paramount here, so he backs out slowly, hoping that he didn't frighten any of them. After all, he is invading their home. The least he can do is leave without a fuss.

By the time he makes it down again, Paprika Sam is panting somewhat alarmingly. Gary frowns and hands him his canteen.

Paprika Sam takes the canteen gratefully and swallows the last couple of gulps.

"Thank you, I desperately needed that," he says with a scratchy voice, which strikes Gary as odd, given he doesn't speak with his actual throat. To be sure, Gary has no idea how this telepathic communication really works. Perhaps dehydration affects areas of his brain, causing the equivalent of hoarseness in the absence of sufficient water. A thought for later.

"I fear to think what has become of your team if even you are in this state."

Paprika Sam grimaces. "If I think about it for too long, it'll only slow me down. No, best to look forward. Where to next, captain?" asks the parched armadillo.

"Next is a creek with tall cliffsides. We may find the peppercorns in cliff swallow's nests, so I will need to commune with the birds. We should be able to get a little water there as well, though it is very muddy."

Paprika Sam observes the cowboy, perhaps wondering how this devastatingly handsome human could convince cliff-nesting swallows to part with anything from their nests voluntarily. Seeming to remember himself, he hastens his steps to follow the man.

They walk for over an hour, and the sun is beginning to yearn toward the western horizon, dipping slightly behind it now. It is still scorching hot and dry as an old man's femur.

By the time they reach the creek bed, they are both sweating so much that neither of them has had to go to the bathroom since they met one another—a frightening sign of severe dehydration.

When they arrive, they make a most disturbing discovery: The creek bed is dry.

"It would appear this year's rains have not come in enough," frowns Peppercorn Gary. "Well, if we don't find it here, we will find the peppercorn in the canyon."

Gary opens the stylish leather satchel on his hip. It features a symbol of a large peppercorn grinder etched onto its surface in dark brown, and is adorned with a horsehair fringe. He pulls out a small flute-like instrument and tests it by blowing into it roughly. Satisfied, he brings it to his lips more gently and plays a tune so beautiful that it brings tears to Paprika Sam's dry eyes.

A swoop of swallows comes barreling out of the many holes of the pocked cliff sides. There are so many at once that the air almost shimmers with their presence, and they all move in a collective swarm that is hypnotic to behold.

As Gary's tune continues, the swallows shift like Moses parting the Red Sea, and from that tunnel emerges a single cliff swallow, its rusty cheeks and dark blue head glinting in the bright sunlight. The creature appears to be carrying something in her delicate claws, and as she gets closer, both Sam and Gary see a small, round shape.

Gary stops his tune and lays the palm of his hand facing up and flat to receive the flighted friend's offering. A small, lumpy, dark blue pebble, in the same metallic shade as the swallow's head. It looks distinctly like a shriveled peppercorn.

After dropping it into Gary's hand, the swallow sings a wistful, trilling note, then flutters away as the others scatter and return to their nests, or to feeding, as they were before.

They both hold their breath as Gary lifts the object to his eyes. He smiles, but it lacks the enthusiasm of one fulfilling their main quest.

"It's what we're looking for, alright, but it's nearly shrivelled to nothing. It could barely help anyone for another half a day, let alone the completion of a project such as yours."

Paprika Sam sags in despair. Gary looks upon him with sympathy and a generous helping of hope. He winks, a half smile adorning his lips, a gold tooth glinting in the bright sunlight.

"This is still good news. It means that the peppercorns will be in the next place, the canyon. The bad news is that the walk there is longer. We will arrive well past sunset. If you can't go on, I still have the energy to dig deep into the earth to find some water for our next trek."

Seeing the need for it, Gary then commences to dig. He digs for so long that the sun begins to set, and the sky lights on fire, casting eruptions of molten colour into the darkening night.

When the light has nearly faded from the sky, Gary exclaims. "Water!" Paprika Sam scrambles over, insomuch as he can in his weak state, and looks down into the hole Gary has dug in the dry creek bed.

"May I lift you into this hole so you can access the water?" asks Gary.

Paprika Sam gives his enthusiastic consent, and the tall cowboy reaches up to gently take the armadillo by his sides, then lowers him into the hole. The armadillo slurps the muddy, meagre water with the gratitude of a child opening all the presents they dreamed of on Christmas morning.

A burst of energy seems to fill him as he begins to dig deeper with a fervor that impresses Gary in no small way. Perhaps armadillos are expert diggers as well. Paleontology was an excellent career choice.

When Sam is finished, he licks his lips and pronounces, "This will keep me going."

Gary takes some of the water into his own dry mouth, nods happily, then climbs out of the hole, lifting the armadillo onto his shoulder.

Just as he is about to put him on the ground again, the armadillo speaks.

"In fact, I rather like it up here, and could use the break. Would you mind carrying me the rest of the way?"

Gary chuckles softly. "Of course, my friend. Your weight is very little to bear."

Paprika Sam smiles gratefully, then rests his head on the man's shoulders, and curls up to sleep.

Peppercorn Gary becomes parched himself and is grateful for the cover of night, which leaches so much less from his dry skin. He slips the shriveled peppercorn into his mouth for what aid it can offer, and right away feels more prepared to continue the journey. They are close now, and salvation is near.

They reach Horsethief Canyon's edge when stars blanket the sky. Streaks of milky way stream across the sky in glowing rivulets, and the night is filled with the gentle sound of cricket song.

Paprika Sam smacks his lips loudly in Peppercorn Gary's ears and lifts his head.

"Have we arrived?" he says in that hoarse voice Gary has become sorely used to.

"We have, my friend. Not much longer now."

He places the armadillo on the ground and removes his backpack once again.

"Now you stay here, and I will rappel down to a secret place where the peppercorns grow. I am trusting you to keep this secret, so please don't let me down."

Paprika Sam nods gravely, then, realizing it is too dark to see, replies, "You have my solemn oath that no other soul will learn of this place from the knowledge you have so graciously bestowed upon me."

Satisfied, Peppercorn Gary secures the hook, then lowers himself down with the rope to a small crevice in the grey, craggy rock. Onlookers would see this as a rock fissure just like any other, a place too narrow for anyone but a mouse to squeeze into. Gary knows better. His ancestors spoke of an offering, of a space widening for those deemed worthy, and Gary knows just the thing to show his worthiness.

From the brim of his hat, he picks off a single peppercorn. Though it pains him to do so, it being one of the last peppercorns his mother gave him before she died, he knows that she would approve. After all, he is doing this to continue the work she died protecting. Though it is a simple black peppercorn, available at any general store, its heavy sentimental value will surely please the guardians of this cove.

He places the peppercorn in front of the cliff face. Sure enough, the fissure opens wider, just enough so that someone of his slim frame can squeeze in. He does so and side steps his way through the opening.

The fissure opens up more as he walks through, and he can use his arms now to push himself along more quickly, knowing that time is of the essence. He hopes dearly that Paprika Sam's team is doing alright.

As he continues, water starts to trickle down the walls of rock, and velvety green moss grows in increasing volume. He even hears the eerie syrinx song of birds. Thrushes, from the sound of it. Grey-cheeked.

The crevice widens considerably, and for the first time since he heard about it as a boy, Gary witnesses the Cerulean Grove, just as his ancestors predicted. A thrill rushes down his spine at the thought that he is the first of his line to see this in a hundred years, and that it still appears to have remained hidden, or at least unharmed.

He looks around, wishing he had more time to take it in, but knowing that he must hurry and find the Cerulean Peppercorn plants.

There is a fine balance, he knows, between showing the gratitude necessary to properly honour and continue to access this place, and finding what he came for in due time. He knows that he can't rush this, so he finds that special place in his consciousness where every moment feels like a lifetime, where every detail in his surroundings becomes so rich to his senses that he can scarcely believe he is on the mortal plane. The soft flutter of thrush wings, the earthy smell of damp soil, the vivid pop of greens, blues, purples, browns, of all the colours around him. He takes the time owed to this sacred place.

Only then do the peppercorn plants pop out to him. They are as his ancestors described: Long, slender, and silverish leaves grow along the branches. Behind many of the leaves along the branches dangle streams of Cerulean peppercorns, their strands swaying gently in a soft breeze. Their bright, blue-green colour sparkles in the filtered light of the secret grove, and Gary is momentarily breathless with wonder. He decides that his ancestors didn't, couldn't, do justice to describe the degree of beauty this plant holds, then remarks on the limitations of any mortal tongue to master descriptions of such majesty.

There are hundreds of peppercorns here, and Gary feels that he has been accepted by the grove. Not only because of his lineage, but because even through dire circumstances, he took the time to appreciate the meaning of this place. The grove also must know that his intentions here are noble, otherwise he wouldn't have been admitted.

Gary fills one of his small draw purses with the peppercorns, promising to return to the grove someday. The grove listens.

It is difficult to leave this place, knowing that long, long ago, his ancestors walked these very steps. But he knows that lives hang in the balance, so he makes his way back through the entrance. It closes behind him, once more a simple fissure in the rock, just like its numerous cousins.

When he climbs back to the top of the canyon, he finds Paprika Sam barely conscious.

With haste, he takes one of the peppercorns from his bag and places it on the armadillo's tongue, closing his mouth around it gently.

He waits, and waits, then waits some more, sitting back on his heels.

Just as his eyes begin to well up with grief, he hears the armadillo swallow in the great silence of the canyon. His breath catches.

Moments later, the armadillo blinks his eyes open, and Gary notices that they look brighter than they have since he met the small scientist.

"So you found them," says the deep, melodic voice once again in his head. It sounds more robust than ever before. "My my, what a miraculous seed!"

Peppercorn Gary laughs, and laughs some more. He didn't realize how much his new friend's wellbeing mattered to him, and now that he has secured it, the relief leaves him feeling somewhat hysterical.

"So it is," he replies in a shaky voice.

The two sit there, gathering themselves for a few peaceful moments before heading to the dig site.

"We can't wait until morning," says Paprika Sam. "Do you mind walking through the night to save my people?"

Peppercorn Gary shakes his head. "Not at all. I can generally function on a few restless nights, and I wouldn't be able to sleep anyway, knowing that your people are in danger."

The armadillo archaeologist smiles. "Follow me."

They walk a long time, until light just begins to show in the east, and end up at the intersection of many rough dirt paths, all worn down with hooves and wheels. At the centre lies an open dig site, filled with bones. Structures have been built around the hole, and many tables covered by rough canvas tents litter the area. Each table is covered with equipment to analyze the bones upon them: delicate brushes, saws, measuring devices. Gary can't name all of the things he sees, and feels humbled by his ignorance.

The others must have tried to escape the heat because none of them are visible. White canvas tents are scattered around the site, and Paprika Sam leads Gary to the one nearest. He calls to the person sleeping inside before entering. A female voice calls back, "Enter." They do.

They enter to see a woman lying prone on a rough cloth mattress and pallet. Her skin is pale and wan, and her voice is gravelly and difficult to hear.

Paprika Sam looks to Gary, who withdraws his drawstring purse and hands the armadillo one of the Cerulean peppercorns. He takes it to the ailing woman and crouches before her.

"Dr. Marlaina Smith, my friend here has brought us a remedy to this affliction we find ourselves with. Please eat this peppercorn. You will feel immediate relief."

She takes the peppercorn in her mouth without hesitation and laboriously swallows the thing, her Adam's apple bobbing as she does so. It seems to get stuck in her throat partway because she begins to cough violently, then it subsides and goes down past her esophagus.

Just like for Paprika Sam, the effect is amazingly fast. The colour returns to her face, and the sweaty sheen, while still there, looks like more of a glow than a pallor. She pushes herself up to standing. Without any formality, she leaves the tent, beckoning for them to follow her.

"We need to revive the others right away. Some of them were very close to death by the time I finally collapsed. I am afraid to see how they are doing now."

In the growing morning light, Paprika Sam and Peppercorn Gary see that some of the academics didn't make it to their tents to rest. They lay on the earthen ground, lips pale and eyes tightly shut, bodies alarmingly limp. Sam takes action.

"Gary, give us each a few peppercorns. We can divide and conquer."

Once they all have some peppercorns, they set off in opposite directions, covering the most ground as quickly as possible. The symmetry of their movements efficiently revives the team, and soon the sounds of harsh breathing and the odd groan turn to sighs of relief and shouts to bring more peppercorns to their fallen colleagues.

By the time the sun is nearly above the horizon, everyone is standing on their own two feet, and some have left with supplies to secure sources of water.

Dr. Smith beams at Peppercorn Gary and Paprika Sam. "Sam, I don't know how you found this mysterious person, or how you came to find this miracle resource, but we can't thank you enough. We thought we were going to die! And just before making a breakthrough."

Paprika Sam's eyes light up.

"You mean you've proven that the males aren't relatives? And that they raised flaplings together?"

"Yes!"

Peppercorn Gary intervenes before this academic discussion can get too involved. "I beg your pardon, but I'd appreciate it if you and your team could keep the 'miracle cure' a secret. Like you, I am on a mission to uncover important information, and for the time being, I would like to keep it hidden while I continue to make discoveries."

They both look at him, somewhat dazed as they withdraw their minds from the heat of academic fervour. As Paprika Sam's eyes clear, his expression changes to one of understanding. "Right, of course, just as we agreed."

Dr. Smith has questions, however. "Why ever would you want to hide such a miracle?"

Peppercorn Gary shuffles awkwardly. "As people who believe in the free exchange of knowledge, I think you can appreciate that some knowledge can be...dangerous, if in the wrong hands. I have very good reason to believe this. Many other similar discoveries I have made would alert a certain interested party to information they would undoubtedly exploit, to the detriment of all that is good and holy."

The two academics nod slowly, understanding dawning. In their work, they have uncovered the secrets of ancient beings that came hundreds of millions of years before a particular rival party believed the world to have even existed. Their current predicament speaks loudly of the implications of that rivalry. For that reason, Paprika Sam and Dr. Smith go from a slow nod to a very deep, fast nod.

"We understand entirely," said Dr. Smith soberly. "I will get our bursar to write up a nondisclosure agreement and get them all to sign it. I won't refer to the peppercorns directly in the agreement, keeping things very vague."

"Thank you for that," says Peppercorn Gary. "Some day in the future, I hope to bring all these findings to the wider public, but there is much I need to do first."

The two get back into their academic discussion and throw around technical terms like "the size of their mandibles" and "groin grooves," until finally Gary asks them what it is they came here to learn.

Dr. Smith lights up like a beacon. "We discovered that some pterosaurs were gay!" she says with great joy.

Peppercorn Gary smiles. He suddenly feels a great kinship with the ancient winged beings. With that discovery tucked away in his satchel, he rides off into the beckoning day in search of truth and peppercorns.

TUNNEL

By Erin Carter

My name is Marcie, and I am the second-best spider killer in Class 10-C. It's cold and getting dark. I curse the cold, and I curse the dark, and I curse the pale pink light cast by the setting sun and the fabric water bag that slops its contents over my hands. If Bear Arms were helping me to carry the untainted water from the ravine to our bunk, then maybe I wouldn't mind so much that my hands are wet and that my legs hurt and that there are rocks in my shoes again. She would be chattering about whether the sky is flamingo or champagne or amaranth or maybe *orchid* pink, and I would be nodding along and pretending to care, instead of praying that I learn to find the same delight in discomfort that she had. Bear Arms made talking about the weather into an art. She wanted to be an interior designer and could chatter about colour for hours. Her arms were covered in doodles that she'd made in permanent marker and highlighter, partially covered by the thick blonde hair that had determined her nickname.

But Bear Arms is dead.

If she were alive then I wouldn't be carrying this water towards the school gymnasium and towards her bunk, which is empty, and to her blankets, which I must wash so that someone else can use them.

Here's one of my last memories of Bear Arms. On Day 247, everyone in Class 10-C who'd passed their midterms were sent through the Rift for some spider killing. There were eight of us. We walked in pairs along the packed snow trail towards the baseball pitch where the Rift hummed and crackled, while Class 10-A and 10-B watched us from the school windows. My boots rubbed my ankles and the air bit my face. Bear Arms skipped alongside me in her bright orange running shoes and Tunnel, hearing the syncopation of her feet on snow, flashed her a jagged smile that made me want to slap her across the face. Then I wanted to slap myself for wanting to slap Tunnel.

Tunnel's name supposedly came from the place where she'd killed her first spider— the stretch of LRT passage between Grandin and Corona. However, I've always thought that it's far more likely that the moniker came from her lips and gums, which were turning black from a fungal infection. It was like looking into the void of space every time she opened her mouth. Her lips and gums were black like a dog's gums, and her teeth were mottled with yellow and black. I wanted to punch each tooth out one by one every time she talked to Bear Arms or me. (Don't misunderstand me. I respect Tunnel. It's impossible not to respect anyone who, upon encountering a spider tenacious enough to get as far East from the Rockies as Edmonton, pulls its legs off and drives pencils through its eyes. But that kind of person is also impossible to like.) Despite her mouth, however, Tunnel was incredibly beautiful, with light, almost white hair which she kept in two braids, and pale eyebrows and thighs like blades.

As I walked, I twirled my cutter, its weight soothing, my cycling gloves wickedly grippy. Bear Arms had her picker strapped to her back, which was technically against the rules since we were supposed to have our tools in hand at all times, but the chances of spiders making it to the Michael A. Kostek were low. Besides, Bear Arms was fast enough that she could unstrap and still catch spiders, pinning them to the ground with the six serrated jaws of the picker, pincers perfectly slotted into the clefts between legs on the cephalothorax, joy on her face as she waited for me to slice off each limb.

"You're staring at Bear Arms' ass again," said Feather.

"I'm not!" I insisted too quickly.

"Wish Feather and I were as close as you and Bear Arms," said Arnica, in a tone that seemed sly. She kept her picker out and ready, skimming it across the snow, occasionally drawing spider prints with the sharp hooks.

I twisted my wrist, arcing my cutter in a mildly threatening way. Mine was steel, much better than the iron tools the rest of the class had. It was a bit of a bummer, actually, having such a nice implement, knowing that if anything happened to me the school board would be more distraught over the loss of the weapon than the loss of my life.

Bear Arms leapt along the crust of snow and past the line of students to Merideth, who stood at first base. We'd dropped the "Ms." from "Ms. Merideth" four months ago, when the curriculum had changed from Math and English and Resource Extraction to Defeating the Arachnid Threat. She hadn't objected to losing her honorific, hadn't even seemed to notice.

Bear Arms had her jacket tied around her waist. Her bear necklace flashed in the winter sun. Finger-shaped bruises constellated her upper arms. Tunnel watched me tracking Bear Arms, smiling her horrid obsidian grin and playing with her utility knife, cutter grasped loosely with her other hand. I avoided eye contact.

"Come on, Mossy," said Tunnel. She was the only one who called me that. To everyone else I was Moss, my field name, or Marcie, my real name. "Smile. You have a chance of beating my kill count today. Aren't you excited? My MRE is yours if you can kill more 'nids." My face burned. I said nothing.

"I'll get to it," Merideth was saying to Bear Arms by the time we approached, "once everyone is here. Alright, 10-C. Jennifer just asked a good question. You're gone for four hours this time. The Rift should drop you off at Site C." A groan rose up from all of us. We hated Site C. Site C was a hole in the side of a mountain. And Site C was dangerous, surrounded by unstable cliffs that sloughed off great slabs of rock without warning. Last year a chunk of granite had fractured off the mountain and crushed a twelfth grader, and her partner had been crippled by a rogue flyrock. "Save it," said Merideth, looking uncharacteristically angry. Her eyes were swollen and her hair was collected into a messy ponytail that looked like it hadn't been brushed. "That's where the Rift is going today. You know I can't do anything about it. Now, once you get off you walk east along the highway until you come to"—she consulted her notes—"a parked semi. The nest is somewhere around there."

"A nest," Tunnel breathed. She jiggled on her heels. She was the only one who looked excited. Bear Arms rubbed her stomach.

"A nest?" said Beetle, saying what we were all thinking. "Merideth, we haven't been tested on dealing with a nest."

"I know," said Merideth. "But you'll do fine. You are all incredibly skilled. We have the highest kill count in the school district, remember, and 10-C ranks highest in speed and agility. After you exterminate the nest, the Rift will reopen at Site D and will stay open all night. Everyone understand?" We all did. "Tunnel, you lead the way with your partner."

"About the partners," said Tunnel. "Have you thought any more about a reassignment?"

"You'll stay with the partner you've been practicing with."

"But wouldn't it make sense to pair the strongest picker with the fastest cutter—"

"Tunnel! You'll go first with your partner."

"Alright," said Tunnel, glowering. "Come on, Yanchyk." She grabbed an unresisting Yanchyk on the upper arm and the two girls disappeared, leaving the smell of metal and conifer behind them as the Rift split and shut again. The rest of 10-C followed, until only Bear Arms and Merideth and I were left.

"But Merideth," said Bear Arms, "Nests are grade twelve. We haven't—"

"You'll be fine," said Merideth. But it was clear from her swollen face that she was lying.

Bear Arms' blankets are surprisingly dirty. They turn the water in the basin pink and then brown. I lather them with a powdery white soap in the showers adjoining the gymnasium. The gymnasium is where we eat and sleep, and it is part of Michael A. Kostek, an elementary school-turned-training base on the west side of Edmonton. The lockers and water fountains are ludicrously small—not meant for high school students, but we were told that none of the high schools in Edmonton were safe for habitation.

None of us had been to Michael A. Kostek before four months ago, and only Tunnel and Bear Arms and I are from Edmonton. After the first spider outbreaks, the school board transferred the remaining Albertan students to where they would be most useful. For us in Class 10-C, that means Michael A. Kostek, which has a Rift in the baseball pitch to take us to the spiders that the curriculum mandates that we destroy.

"I can finish this," says Tunnel. I hadn't heard her coming up behind me. She begins to knead the blankets. Her bleached braids nearly dip into the soapy water.

"Thanks."

"No problem. Have you seen the schedule yet?"

"No." I haven't looked, don't feel like seeing Bear Arms' name scratched out with Merideth's big black pen.

"You should look." When I get to the schedule, I see that Tunnel and Yanchyk still have the highest kill count. I am in second place, Bear Arms' name beside mine. Not crossed out yet. And we've been assigned to go back through the Rift on Day 249. Tomorrow.

Outside the school windows, the sky looks inflamed. Raw meat pink.

When Bear Arms and I stepped through the Rift on Day 247, it was raining.

"What on God's green earth?" said Bear Arms.

"I don't understand," I said. Rain? In November? It wasn't possible. We stood on a highway strewn with the hulking shapes of abandoned cars, each carpeted in snow. On one side the rock face of the mountain stretched upwards. On the other, a metal guardrail separated us from a sudden drop and the tops of trees. Everyone clustered underneath a rock outcropping, unpacking our waterproof jackets.

I squinted through the rain, looking for rockfall scars. Was I imagining it, or were there significantly more boulders littered along the road, more swathes of crushed trees below?

"We should go back," I said.

"We'll be okay," said Bear Arms. "Merideth wouldn't have sent us if we couldn't do it."

"Oh yes, she would."

"We can't go back, bitches," said Tunnel. "We're here until we find the nest and kill some 'nids, and the Rift re-opens for us. So let's get cracking!

Now that we're here, there's a new plan. The Beetle twins are leading. Mossy and Yanchyk scout ahead. And Bear Arms and I will bring up the rear."

"What if Bear Arms doesn't want to go with you?" I asked.

"But she does, doesn't she?" Tunnel put her arm around Bear Arms' shoulder.

Bear Arms' eyes were as wide as ping pong balls. She gave the tiniest of nods. "I'd love to bring up the rear!

"I'm sorry, Marcie," she said as she hugged me.

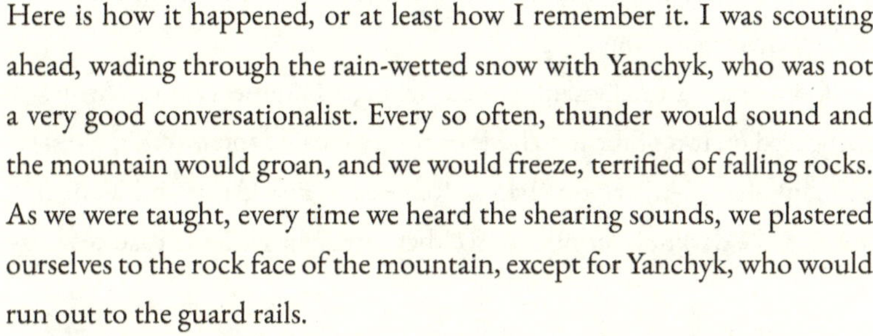

Here is how it happened, or at least how I remember it. I was scouting ahead, wading through the rain-wetted snow with Yanchyk, who was not a very good conversationalist. Every so often, thunder would sound and the mountain would groan, and we would freeze, terrified of falling rocks. As we were taught, every time we heard the shearing sounds, we plastered ourselves to the rock face of the mountain, except for Yanchyk, who would run out to the guard rails.

"You need to stop that," I told her. "It's not safe. More of a chance you'll get hit." She shook her head, pale with terror. "Tunnel!" I called behind me, hoping that she could knock some sense into her partner. Through the rain, I could make out the shapes of the Beetle sisters trudging behind us, and that was it.

"We're nearly there," said Yanchyk. "You don't have to call her. Please, please, let's just go."

"Why are you so scared of her?" I wanted to know.

"Look, we're here," she said. And we were. Merideth was right: there was a semi-truck, but parked was not the word I would have used to describe its position. It was on its side, cab dangling off of the precipice, the guard rail twisted and warped around it.

"But where's the nest?" asked Arnica, arriving behind us.

"I don't get why we're even here. The spiders aren't going to come out if it's raining," said Yellow Beetle. She must have found some mascara a few days ago, because it ran in thick black streaks down her cheeks.

"How do you know?" Arnica asked. "How much do any of us know about the spiders, really? Other than how to kill them."

"Do you hear that?" I asked. It was hard to hear over the rain, but it was there: stridulation, the hissing sound of spiders rubbing their haired legs together.

"Fuck!" said Arnica. My back touched someone else's: we'd clustered in a knot facing outwards. We all peered into the darkness. There was nothing: no movement, nothing.

"Come on," I finally said, voice cracking. "Gimme a boost, Arnie." I clambered on top of the metal side of the semi truck and pulled the rest of 10-C up after me. Everyone had arrived except Bear Arms and Tunnel. I scanned the darkness, hoping to see them straggling up the road towards us.

"They'll be here soon," said Feather. Thunder rolled and a strike of lightning bleached her face for a moment, illuminating her acne-pocked skin and a droplet of water quivering on her nose. "They were right behind me."

"Shit, there it is!" said Yellow Beetle.

"There's what?"

"The nest! Wait for more lightning."

We waited. I hunkered down, my knees touching the slick surface of the semi. There was a sudden rumble and a long metal screeching noise, and then lightning flashed and we all saw what was on the other side of the semi. The highway extended through a tunnel cut into the mountain, and the entrance to the tunnel was thick with webs that reflected lightning. The webs were crawling with spiders, each the size of a small dog or cat.

"Oh damn," said Arnica.

"Yeah," I said. "That's a lot."

"Okay, but there's not much point in being here now though. They're not going to come out when it's raining."

"Unless Merideth wanted us to go into the nest?" said Yellow Beetle. None of us liked that thought very much. We waited for someone to agree that we should go in. No one said anything. There was a third rumble of thunder. The semi began to groan. We scrambled down and plastered ourselves to the side of the mountain. A deep vibration filled my ears and shook my pelvis. There was another long screeching noise— this one a mixture of metal and animal, something inhuman. Inhuman, but familiar. And when the rain thinned, I looked up to see Tunnel walking towards us, her face badly scratched and bleeding, and no Bear Arms.

So that's how it happened. Falling rocks. Falling rocks that Bear Arms—most nimble student in Class 10-C, a cutter so fast that Tunnel coveted her as a partner—could not dodge, that apparently bowled her off the mountain entirely. I sit on Bear Arms' bunk, swinging my legs, and watch Yellow Beetle stretch. Tunnel pulls down Bear Arms' blankets from where they'd been drying, adds them to her own bed. After she told us what happened to Bear Arms, we'd spent the whole time looking for her. We'd returned through the rift without trying to engage the spiders.

But tomorrow, Merideth will send us back to the nest. I will be paired with Tunnel. Yanchyk has run away. I think of the last time I saw her, and the bruises going up her arms, and I think of Bear Arms, with the same bruises. And the bloodstains in her blankets and on her mattress near the headboard. Not where you'd expect bloodstains. And I think of Tunnel flicking her knife, and of Bear Arms, fast in her bright orange running shoes.

Tunnel sits next to me. A bear-shaped necklace glints between her breasts.

"So, you've been assigned as my partner tomorrow," she says.

"I know," I say. "I look forward to it."

And I do. We will stand in front of the tunnel. We will stand on the overturned semi, and wait for the sea of black, furred legs to approach, and then we will do what we are trained to do: pick and cut, slice and immobilize, skewer and sever. The sun will set, blood-red. And I will be the best killer in Class 10-C.

FIVE CLOUDS, A LITTLE TO THE LEFT

BY O.E. FLYNN

On the Thirteen Thousandth, Three Hundred and Ninety-Fourth day of the Frost, the Lord of All Gods, the One Above All, the Almighty came unto the World.

And He despaired.

He saw that Man, the inheritors of the World the Lord had created, had not learned. He remembered the times He had punished Man and they had not listened. He remembered the Great Flood that had drowned their abominations, the Five-and-Five Plagues He had visited upon the Goldstone Empire, the Rains of Salt that poisoned the plains of Syddim for a generation.

He looked upon the World and saw the great plain of white, of winter that Man had created. The frozen hearts and frozen hates, the crimes of Man, their lies and their violations of the World and their trespasses against Him.

They had forgotten the face of their Father.

The Lord of All Gods beheld what had been wrought and knew what must be done.

In the early hours of a slightly different September 26th, 1983, a bank of clouds formed slightly differently than they had during the September 26th, 1983 we are more familiar with. These clouds, five of them, formed slightly left from where they did in the familiar timeline. Five clouds, slightly to the left, lead to nothing of significance occurring on this day. All inhabitants of the Earth carried on without altering their day-to-day activities, but this absence had far-reaching consequences...

Blissfully unaware of any atmospheric and quantum differences, Alexander Rhaim sipped his black coffee and frowned at the burned bean water hitting his tongue. He swallowed it nonetheless, silently musing about the series of unfortunate events that led him to waiting for the man from DC to meet him in the Stonewall Inn's cafe at this ungodly hour. He checked his watch for the seventeenth time since he sat down. 5:47 a.m. on a chilly November Friday. A few more weeks and 1983 would finally be over.

Had he been born a little different, he'd still be sleeping, but as it was... Alex snickered to himself for the thought. His life was never going to be normal, such things flew out the window the day he was born.

A gay black man raised by ex-Panthers, who then had the blind luck to get into university to study the literature of his oppressors to hopefully write a novel that would reveal "It" to the reader. The powers that be, their tools of oppression, and most importantly, how to fight back. "It" had been done before, many times. A largely hopeless endeavour, Alex knew that, but a gay black radical was used to tilting at windmills.

When he wasn't writing, Alex worked at a little hole-in-the-wall bodega on the corner of Bleeker and LaGuardia that served as the public, legitimate side of the NMF, the Neo-Motherfucker Movement. They sold all the usual accoutrements, but also underground music, art supplies, and more than a few pieces of seditious literature. Nothing too crazy, that was their other members' responsibility, but Marx, Louverture, John Brown, and anyone else that would curl Nancy Reagan's hair. That was why he was drinking bad coffee at a gay bar in the Village, waiting for some unknown man from the centre of American imperial power to tell him something that was apparently critical. It felt like a bad spy thriller, something an insurance salesman with too much time on his hands would write.

He wasn't looking forward to explaining to Persephone why he'd taken this risk, but the voice on the phone, even through the vocoder, was too familiar to deny. Besides, she'd already set up a series of decoy locations for him to "disclose" under interrogation. It felt excessive, but he couldn't deny the woman was committed to the NMF (or should be committed).

The NMF started life as a small little anarchist artist commune, specializing in using the absurd to critique the power, much like the group from the '60s that inspired their name. But in recent years, they'd taken on a more active role. Now they used their art as a smokescreen, and their connections to try and bridge the gap between a crapton of other lefty orgs across the US. They did the occasional more public show of dissent—they had an Armistice Day protest planned in solidarity with their brethren in Berlin, who had been in the streets since the seventh.

There were only a dozen of them, but they all were like Alex—an eclectic mix of faggots, pinkos, carpetmunchers, negros, and other damnfool idiots. They did their best to make sure the org's women's libbers, black radicals, gays, angry students, and the allies who just woke up all played nice with one another. It wasn't glamorous, it wasn't flashy, but it was necessary. All their backs were against the wall, it didn't matter the minor differences between them when the drums finally stopped.

Yet another windmill, but you do what you can.

The little bell over the door tinkled again, and Alex turned to see a natty, bespectacled white man enter, looking like a lost little lamb. A little lamb that Alex knew. The guy locked eyes with him, strode over, and sat down.

"Hi Alexander," Francis Miller said, looking handsome in his three-piece tweed suit and silver paisley clip-on bow-tie.

"Hey Franny..." Alex took a moment to recover before continuing. "Gotta say, you were the last person I'd expected to show up here."

Francis—Franny—coughed uncomfortably. "Yes, well our lives took very different directions didn't they?"

Alex scoffed. "Yeah man, you could say that. I didn't know you were working in DC, what're you doing now?"

"I work for the Bureau."

"The fuck you doing here then? You think you can call *me* up after five years and reconnect now that you're a goddamn spook?" Alex shoved a finger toward his own chest. "What good do you think someone like you will do there anyway? You think if you do a good enough job, Uncle Sam will give you a belly rub? Back where I'm from, we got a name for idiots like you."

"Alex, it's not like that."

"No? Tell me how you're different from the folk that thought they could get ahead if they just sucked up to the master of the house enough. You're a goddamn nancy boy working in the *J. Edgar Hoover* building. The man would've lynched a fag like you if he wasn't too busy doing the same to people like me... that and jumping at commies in his goddamn cereal."

Franny didn't flinch this time. Instead he leaned forward and spoke very low, very carefully, in a voice Alex only ever heard in the small hours of the morning when he had his arms wrapped around the man.

"You're right, Alex. Everything you said, you're right. I am what you say I am. I was stupid and I thought that the times were changing and that I could make a difference. Change something like the FBI into something better. But I was wrong. It wasn't until this Tuesday that I realized how wrong. Wednesday, I resigned."

Alex narrowed his eyes. Despite his anger, this was entirely in line with what he expected of Franny. Of course he would think that he, a lone gay man, would be able to change the FBI from within. Of course he, with that white boy arrogance, would try to do some dumbass shit like that. And he would quit in the most dramatic way possible then call up his ex-boyfriend using a vocoder and arrange a meeting at the home of the gay revolution. A stupid, honorable, arrogant man with flair for the dramatic.

Which was why, despite the anger, despite the years, despite everything, Alexander Rhaim still loved him.

Of course.

Alex leaned forward, his face now inches away from Franny's, and whispered back in the tone that he also only used in the small hours of the morning.

"Franny, what happened on Tuesday?"

It was 6:30 in the morning and, if asked, Persephone Tough (pronounced Toe as she had to so often remind her fellows) would have described her mood as "sulfuric" or "willing to commit homicide."

The reason?

Her teatime had been interrupted by the arrival of Alex and some man she did not know. Alex knew better than to interrupt the drinking of her first cup of tea—everyone did. The Emilys were the only exception to this rule. Each, in her turn, had teased Persephone for how grumpy she could get, but Emilys could usually get away with that because of what happened the night before.

The fact that the only three girls she'd fallen for had all been named Emily was not a thing to be considered further nor discussed.

The tea was one of the few truly bourgeois comforts she allowed herself; a lovely imported tea from Harrowgate. The fucking English couldn't make whiskey and nor should they try, but every right-thinking Scot, in her mind anyway, had to admit they could make a good tea. Every other part of her life was spent either studying at Langone or riding herd as the manager of NMF's "cultural liaisons," the nice title for the gaggle of the state's forgotten children that they called a community.

Another comfort was also on the desk at the back of the bodega: Her mother's tarot cards. Another piece of her interrupted morning routine. She'd set out a simple three-card array; nothing too posh. Two were turned over and she had been about to look at the last when Alex barged in her door.

The Wheel of Fortune, inverted, and The Hanged Man, right side up.

Something bad was going down today.

It would have to be today, when most of the NMF was either in Berlin or DC helping organise anti-war protests. It didn't take a genius to see that times were tense between NATO and the Soviets, but that didn't stop either side from rattling the sabre. Fucking Reagan had pushed for the Able Archer games to go ahead, Thatcher invaded the Falklands, Andropov was stomping harder on the Afgans. All of 'em were trying to puff up their chests to show everyone how big and bad they were.

But if there were two things that Berliners were good at doing, it was making more lesbians and protesting. Even the *East Germans* were getting in on the second one.

Apparently, there was a massive crowd on either side of the Wall, all playing music at each other. They weren't stupid, they knew any war would be fought in their country first. No matter who won, Germany wouldn't look the same after. So they got bloody good at registering their dissatisfaction with the situation. Hell, even Nena was there, her latest celeb crush. They'd just finished playing the title track of their newest album.

Fewer things better in this world than a punk rock girl with messy dark hair, screaming her lungs out at the man.

But, apparently, there was no time to worry about that now. She took a sip of her tea, swallowed, swung her heavy combat boots onto her desk, and glared at Alex and the deeply uncomfortable looking suit across from her. Neither of the two men who darkened her door this morning seemed like they were interrupting her on a lark, so she chose to restrain her justifiably murderous rage to merely thinking dark thoughts about them rather than carrying them out.

"Alright, Alex. Care to tell me why exactly you have decided to interrupt my morning routine this day? The penalty for such an infraction has been noted and I will expect recompense at your earliest convenience." Nobody gets in the way of teatime without bringing her chocolate, especially not this early in the morning. "This had better be damned good. And who the fuck is this?"

But as she looked at Alex, someone she had seen throw bricks at cops more than a few times and not even blink, she realized how fucking scared he looked. His normally clear, shiny dark skin was sallow, lifeless.

"Pers, this is Franny. We met at school a couple of years ago." Alex gestured at his companion.

She motioned for him to continue.

"We met up today and... he told me... We're fucked, Pers!"

Ma's cards never miss.

"Hold up." She looked at the suit. "Franny, is it? The fuck is Alex banging on about? And why the fuck did he bring you here of all places? You're so starched, you have to have come from Washington."

Franny (Francis?) shifted uncomfortably where he stood. "Umm... I'm sorry ma'am. I worked for the FBI—"

"Alex!" Persephone suddenly found herself on her feet, papers and pencils scattering everywhere. "What in the *god damn fuck* are you thinking bringing a *copper* here?"

Surprisingly, Alex seemed to recover his courage at this barrage. "Stop it, he's not the problem! It's the Feds! They're coming for us, Pers. Franny quit because he saw my name on the warrant. He came here to warn me, to warn us."

Her head swiveled over to Franny. "This true?"

He (somehow) stiffened even further. "Yes, ma'am. They're under the impression you people are some kind of communist guerilla force, another May 19th Coalition. They've got SWAT, armoured cars, the whole deal. They're going to go in, guns blazing, and arrest anyone who isn't dead afterwards."

Well, this qualifies as Very Important.

"When?" she asked him.

"This afternoon, 5:00 p.m. When you're doing your Armistice Day broadcast. The Deputy Director wants to have a good catch for the President when he gets back from Japan."

Her mind whirred, locking into place long dormant plans and countermeasures. But before she could set them into motion, she leaned over her desk and fixed her gaze on Alexander. He was slumped into a chair, head in hand.

She had to be certain.

"And you trust this man?"

"Yeah, Pers." He didn't meet her gaze, lost in the fog of despair.

"Alexander," she pressed. "I need you to look me in the eye."

He complied. His eyes were red, tears streaming down his face.

"Pers, he quit his job to warn me. It all lines up. It has to be true."

"Yeah, why? 'Cause yer star-crossed lovers? A gay anarchist and a government spook, never a tale of more woe?" she asked.

Alex snorted, before looking at Franny. "Yeah, something like that."

"Touching, truly..." her last word drifted as her mind raced.

The last piece now slotted into place, all criteria met. So it was now or never. She opened the bottom drawer of her desk and removed the false bottom. Inside was a flat safe with two locks.

"I am activating the Jackboot Protocol. Alex, do you concur with my assessment of the situation?"

"Yeah..." he wiped his face and steadied himself, his voice taking on a much more formal tone. "Yes, as the situation does not permit us to contact anyone else, I agree. You may proceed with the Jackboot Protocol."

He handed his key to her and she pulled out her own and slotted each into the small safe. Inside there were a dozen envelopes with a Canadian passport and fifteen hundred US dollars in each; one for every member of the NMF. Alongside them was a folded piece of paper, a dusty revolver, and a box of .38 caliber bullets. She passed eleven of the envelopes to Alex, who placed them in a duffle bag. The last she left on her desk.

"I'm sorry, Francis, I don't have one for you. And you and Alex aren't going to see each other for a long time. They'll be watching you for this, if they aren't already. Don't use phones to contact anyone you care about for at least six months. Once you're certain you have shaken the heat for at least a year, go to Canada. Nova Scotia is lovely, basically colder Newark."

Francis looked like he had been hit on the head with an anvil. "What is all of this?"

"Don't blame me. Pers is one who's chronically paranoid, it was all her idea," Alex spoke up while Persephone double checked the pistol. Six rounds loaded, another two dozen in the box. She clipped the holster to her belt as she shook her head.

"I'm not paranoid, Alexander. I'm prepared. You're lucky I'm not so petty to remind you that I'm also right."

"So you are some kind of cell?" Francis sputtered. "Bundles of money, fake passports, and a gun?"

Persephone glared at him and then to Alex, who jumped in again. "Hold up, Pers! No, Franny, not in the slightest. All we do, all we've ever done is help people organize, talk with one another, keep the lines open. We organize protests, send letters. Nothing more than that."

"Then why are they after you, Alex? Why do you have all this stuff?"

"You tell me!" he bellowed back. "The Feds are the ones—"

Cli-click.

Both men turned to her as Persephone pulled back the hammer and pointed the revolver at Francis.

"I'm going to have to ask you to settle down now, Francis. And listen up, because you've got a fucking big decision to make about how the next few minutes go." Her heart pounded but the anger kept her voice steady. "You should know, better than anyone here, that the FBI, the CIA, MI5, and all the other spook orgs have been cracking down on us lefties here for nigh on three decades now. They've infiltrated, divided, diminished and done everything else in their power to keep us from even seeing each other as human beings, while they let the neo-Nazis and the Klan and all the other racists go without so much as a tap on the nose. We're a threat because the state sees us that way. No other reason. Now you're *here,* which means that you've made one good choice so far. So I'll give you one chance to make another."

"Pers, no!" Alex hissed.

"When I point a gun at someone, Alexander, I mean to use it." Her eyes never left the suit. "This ain't personal, there's just no middle ground here, Francis. You're either a dangerous homosexual or you're a government cunt come to lock away the dangerous homosexuals, yeah? Nothing in between. You can help us get the word out to those that depend on us, or I shoot you right now. Now, what'll it be?"

She could see the sweat dripping down his face, the slight tremble in his body, but when he spoke his voice was clear and measured.

"I made my choice before I came to Alex. I guess that makes me... a dangerous homosexual. One who is very sorry for losing his nerve for a moment. How can I help?"

Persephone made her own choice. She safetied the gun and holstered it. "Good man."

"Goddamn it, Persephone." Alex let out a long breath. "Don't fucking do that again or *I'll* shoot you."

"I'd like to see you try," she fired back. "You can't do anything straight, much less shoot. Now quit your whining and get the wireless going. Take the sheet and start broadcasting on all those channels. Franny, go help him, you two can bond over how much you hate the scary Scottish lesbian. I'll apologise later if you don't fuck us over."

Franny still looked stunned. "Wha... what are you going to do?"

"I'm going down to the boiler room with every scrap of paper we got, shove it into the furnace, then turn the fucker up as high as she'll go. I told you, we ain't waiting around for the spooks to get us and ours." She pocketed the last tarot card, making sure to keep the orientation the same, but not daring to look until everything was finished.

Five minutes later she was exactly where she said she would be, three-twentieths of the way through the lighter-fluid-covered files. She heard Alex shouting. She couldn't make it out. The FBI was probably going mental, maybe they were already on the way. Nothing she could do about that, so she just started shoveling papers in faster.

Four-twentieths, then six, then halfway done. Nearly there.

"Persephone! Get your ass up here!"

"Fuck," she muttered to herself more than anything.

Taking the stairs three at a time, she ran to the makeshift radio room they'd made in the broom closet of the bodega. Alex was hunched over the ham radio, with Franny looking down at him as he frantically switched frequencies back and forth. Both of them had headphones connected. But he wasn't talking. She frowned.

"What is it?"

Alex didn't even turn around, instead just flicked a switch. "Listen."

The bodega intercom crackled to life as a man's voice spilled out. She couldn't understand the language, but he was clearly in distress. Every third word seemed to quiver, and every so often a sob came out. There was gunfire and other men shouting in the background, but the strange transmission continued.

"...yeslii vui eto slushite, oo vas astalos' men'she chasa, chtob' v'bratsya. Raisa? Dimitrii? Ya lublu vas oboikh. Ya lublu—"

Gunfire again, then only static. She looked at the two men, incredulous.

"The fuck am I listening to, Alex?"

"I don't know, but it's on at least a half dozen frequencies." Alex frowned as he fiddled with the dials. "It's not a number station jammer either. That's gotta be a message of some kind."

"Alex..." Franny's voice trembled. "Alex, that's Russian... It has to be the Soviets."

Persephone's mind raced. "What the fuck are the goddamn Russkies doing on my airwaves?"

The speakers started up again with the same man's voice. The gunfire was dying down, only occasionally bursts coming through. Softer shouts from people in the background could also be heard, but over all of that, as calmly as he could, the man spoke again. This time in English.

"Hello, this is Lieutenant-Colonel Simon Petrov of the Moscow Oblast Air Defense Force. Thirty-five minutes ago, at approximately 1:13 p.m., local time, our ground based radar detected the launch of approximately one hundred nuclear capable missiles from the area around West Berlin.

Before such a launch could be independently confirmed, our political officer triggered Perimeter. I shot him shortly after that, but it was too late—"

Another burst of gunfire interrupted him.

"Tovarisch Komandir!" Starshina Gennady Shukov shouted. "It would appear the Chekists are at it again."

Lieutenant Colonel Simon Pentrov disengaged the radio receiver in his hand and tried to keep his voice from shaking as he yelled back.

"Seal the door! Don't let them through, Comrade Master Sergeant."

Gennady didn't respond. He didn't need to. They'd served together for five years and Petrov knew he could count on the man to do his duty. He gathered the remainder of his squad together, all twenty of them, and fired a burst down the hall while *efreitors* Yaroslav and Miroslav Istchenko, big Ukrainian farm boys, shoved the blast door of their command bunker. As it slowly closed, Petrov clicked the radio back on and started over.

"To anyone receiving me, this is Lieutenant Colonel Simon Petrov, transmitting in the clear from AvtoKom Bunker Zero-Two, deep under Moscow. Thirty-five minutes ago, our early warning satellites registered one hundred nuclear launches originating from West Berlin. Fifteen minutes from now, our automated response system, Perimeter, will launch all Soviet silo based missiles in response to what is seen as an existential threat to the Soviet Union."

Petrov clicked off the receiver and took a breath, then another. The sergeant approached and he met Gennady's gaze, who simply nodded to him. They were sealed in here. It would take the Spetsnaz days to get through that door. The base intercom panel lit and an angry, commanding voice blared at them before the sergeant turned it down, listening intently.

"The good general wishes to know what's going on, Comrade Colonel," Gennady called over. "What should I say?"

"Distract them please, Sergeant Shukov. At your discretion."

While Petrov could no longer hear the Spetsnaz commander, he did hear Shukov's... liberal interpretation of his orders.

"Ah, Comrade General. Apologies, we had a, uh, a minor weapons malfunction. But we are fine, we're all fine here, now. Thank you, Comrade General. How are you?"

If the world was not about to end, Master Sergeant Gennady Shukov would have been shot once they realized he was quoting an imperialist film. But luckily for him, Commissar Tupolev now lay in a puddle of his own blood less than a metre away from the communications console. Petrov spat on the body before continuing his broadcast.

"Our political officer panicked. He did not wait for confirmation and against my advice, triggered the automated system. The Chekist locked himself in the control room and shot four of my men before I could get in. By then it was too late. The command missile left its silo ten minutes ago and my remaining men and I can do nothing to stop the rest of the launches. Nothing but this."

He tried to take another steadying breath, but Petrov couldn't stop the tears from flowing. He kept thinking of Raisa, his wife, and his son Dimitri. She'd be bringing him home from school, maybe she would go see Anya, Gennady's wife.

Maybe, somehow, they would turn on the radio, hear him and run. They were broadcasting on as many frequencies as they could, maybe... He forced himself to keep talking.

"The system is set to counter-value, to behave as though NATO has attacked via surprise and there is no way to stop your launch or your invading forces. The targets in this scenario are chosen to assure full destruction of the enemy over preventing further military action. Major cities, farmland, industrial centres!" He was shouting, anger and frustration steeling his voice. "You have until approximately 2:45 p.m. before the missiles finish fueling and launch. Between 3:00 and 3:15 p.m., they will begin landing."

He heard Gennady curse and fire his weapon into the comms panel.

"Dull conversation anyway... Comrade Colonel, we are about to have company!"

We're dead already. A loud bang cracked through the room, sounding like cannons in the outer halls. *Fuck Secretary Andropov, Brezhnev, Gorbachev, and all those old men in the Presidium. Fuck the KGB, the GRU, and all the other Chekists. Fuck their rickety empire and every last idiots who brought us here. They do not deserve my faith.*

"Most of the weapons that will be fired at Europe will be R-twelve model intermediate range missiles with an explosive power of two-and-a-half megatons. According to my systems, more than fifteen hundred are being prepared. Their minimum safe distance is twelve kilometers and they will be deployed in a full saturation pattern against all major European cities over 100,000 people. This means you must be at least twelve kilometers outside city limits in order to have a chance to survive. It is unlikely your systems will be able to intercept them, so your only choice will be to run. Flee to the south, Morocco, Turkey, anywhere across the Mediterranean.

"In America, you will be targeted by approximately three hundred R-thirty-six intercontinental ballistic missiles. Two-hundred fifty are multi-payload, containing ten 550 kiloton warheads along with a minimum of forty penetration aids and decoys. Once those have been deployed, they will become much harder to destroy so your best chance is to scramble your interceptors now and prepare your ABM systems immediately to destroy them at their apogee. The remaining missiles are single warhead, twenty *megatons* devices, upgraded with a cobalt sheath and set to low altitude detonation. This is to maximize the amount and duration of radioactive fallout they produce. There can be no minimum safe distance for anyone in America. Flee to Mexico or Cuba to avoid the worst of the radiation."

Another crack, but the door held. It was designed to withstand a direct nuclear strike. A third explosion, and then a fourth. The GRU Spetsnaz might as well have been setting off Christmas crackers in a metal drum. By some strange twist of fate, they sounded nearly musical.

"If... if anyone in NATO military command is listening, please know this is a mistake. I know you will have to retaliate, but please, if you can find it in your hearts, stop your launch or limit the damage as much as you can. This is not an act of spite, this is a result of our collective fear and paranoia of one another. We can no longer stop this, but your response is in your hands."

The pounding on the door stopped, finally.

"To my comrades, in the air, at sea, and in the republics, if you are asked to launch more weapons, if you are ordered to your planes, please refuse. I know what I am asking. I know it will cost you your lives. But the world we knew is already dead with what will be launched. So every bomb that does not drop, every plane that does not take off, every submarine that remains docked, means that thousands of lives are saved. There is no need to add more suffering out of spite. This day, we are all comrades. East and West don't matter anymore. Only life."

He clicked on the receiver one last time.

"To everyone else out there, I am sorry. I am so sorry. I hope you can get away, to make your escape. That you will live." He choked off a sob. "It is now 1:56 p.m., Moscow Standard Time. The missiles will be in the air in forty-nine minutes. Good luck and may God have mercy on all of us. This is Lieutenant-Colonel Simon Petrov, signing off."

That is it. That is all I can do. He clicked the receiver off as Gennady put a hand on his shoulder.

"It has been an honor, Comrade Petrov."

Persephone stared at Alex and Franny, too stunned to speak. The only sound that filled the bodega was static from the speakers. Alex was frozen with his hand on the radio, Franny holding his other hand while sitting on the desk. Three minutes passed.

Alex broke the silence first.

"Pers?" His voice sounded like it was coming from another world. "What do we do?"

Her brain simply spun uselessly, like slamming the accelerator down while the car was in neutral. She had no plan for this, every existing scheme seemed so useless, so small now.

How do you stop something like this? What the fuck do you do?

"Pers?" Alex asked again.

She stared blankly at him, gears still flinging themselves about, bouncing off the inside of her skull.

"We could run," Franny spoke up. "My car's outside, but it would take us forty minutes or more just to get to the highway. We might get lucky, though."

That did it. Persephone's mind finally found its footing and roared back to life. She reached into her pocket and turned the last card over. The Star, upright.

Hope, rebirth, rejuvenation.

The Jackboot Protocol. She didn't need to burn the books anymore, but the rest of it would work just fine. That Russkie colonel had the right idea.

Hope.

"Franny, take Alex and get out of here. We follow our new friend's instructions. Take the passports, all the money and the gun. I'm sure you can pick the safest route to Canada. Don't stay long. Nuclear winter will not be good up there, but it'll be a safer place to find a boat to Mexico."

Francis looked like he was about to argue, but the former FBI man wasn't stupid. He knew what was going on and simply nodded.

"I'll look after him. If Colonel Petrov is correct, we'll go to Montana. Counter-value priority means they won't be after the silos there, so we can get to Alberta or Saskatchewan safely. My car has a phone too, we'll be able to contact people as we drive."

"God be with ya on that. The phone lines will be jammed with panic soon enough, but try anyway. Move yer ass, Alex." Glasgow started returning more to her voice as she shoved him out of his chair and sat down. "Plans are changing and yer posh boyfriend is taking you on a vacation to the colonies. Franny, don't let him drive, he's real bad at it. But he can cook, so get him to make you his famous French toast before all the food runs out."

Alex dumbly complied as Franny took hand.

"Wait a sec!" Alex protested, finally shaking off the shock then spinning to face Persephone. "I haven't agreed to go anywhere. And what the fuck are *you* going to do?"

"Don't argue with me, Alexander." She checked her pocket watch, a gift from her father for getting accepted at NYU. "You've got forty-four minutes before those birds are in the air. Don't waste 'em!"

That was a mistake, looking at the watch.

Her thoughts strayed from the Plan, her mind calculating other statistics. Glasgow, her home, 1.7 million people, a primary target. Ma and Da, sixty-three this year, living in Rutherglen, five kilometres from Glasgow. Da'd be napping in his favorite chair after lunch. Ma'd be doing a crossword.

They didn't drive, of course. Why would you need to?

English Emily, Emily Critchley, the first Emily... she'd be working. Downtown Slough at 2:00 p.m., 100,000 people. Upwind from London, but nowhere close to safe. The streets would be packed.

Emily Schreiber was at the Nena concert in Berlin, nearly three million people over both sides of the Wall. In minutes, the whole city would be ash. She'd be lucky if the air raid sirens even had time to go off.

The last Emily, Emily Flores, had the best chance. San Francisco, three quarters of a million people, would have the longest warning... if anyone there heard it.

We heard it.

Franny gently but firmly placed his hand on Alex's bicep, trying to guide him out of the closet. Alex almost let him.

"Pers, come with us. We can all go together."

"No."

She couldn't look at him, the tears were starting. So she sat down and started fiddling with the radio.

"What do you mean, no?"

"Alex, don't..." Franny whispered. "She's staying."

"No! Why? What the fuck do you think you're going to do here?"

"The same thing I was planning to do before. The same thing Mr. Petrov risked everything to do. Tell our friends and anyone else who will listen what's about to happen and get them out. As I said, the hardlines will probably go down soon, but this baby'll last until the power goes."

Alex made to grab her, but Franny stopped him, trapping him in a tight embrace. He glanced wildly at him before looking back at her. She kept her gaze pointedly forward; she didn't want him to see her cry.

"Don't make this harder than it has to be, Alexander. There's lots to say, but there's only one radio. I don't need help with this. Save yourselves, this Motherfucker can keep the lights on herself."

"Pers..." he whispered. "It don't gotta be you."

She shook her head, tears staining the paper on the desk.

"It can *only* be me, Alex. You have someone to live for, a hope, and a chance, slim as it is. My whole family's going to die and there's not a goddamn thing I can do about it. Everything I've dedicated my life to is about to go up in smoke." She finally turned to him. She knew she looked pathetic, but she owed him this at least. "But this? I can do this. I can try, I don't know if it'll matter in the end, but I can try. That's all I can do."

Alex ripped himself out of Franny's grasp and stepped towards her, before pulling her into a massive hug. She laughed before dissolving into sobs entirely. She felt him shift and his deep voice rumble in his chest.

"Franny, get the fuck in here, man."

Three dangerous homosexuals embraced for one last time. After a few moments, Persephone pushed them apart.

"Go," she told them.

Alex was crying and only nodded. Francis took his hand and smiled.

"Thank you, for everything."

"Don't forget it, either of you. Find another scary Scotch lesbian and give her the chocolate you owe me."

It took only two more minutes for the squeal of tires on asphalt to greet her ears. Persephone Tough let herself cry for one more minute after that before forcing it all down and steadying herself. She recovered her cup of tea, tied her hair back, and set up the old record player just outside the broom closet. Thumbing through the vinyls, she thought about Colonel Petrov and his men.

What would they *want to hear? What would help them keep their courage in this horrid time?*

They'd never hear it, but it comforted her to imagine that they somehow would. That this tiny act would help them, somehow. Some vibration through the world to keep them safe for all they did, all they lost. She thumbed through her battered collection.

She briefly considered throwing on her bootleg recording of the USSR's national anthem, partially out of respect but also to piss off the FBI, who were undoubtedly still monitoring her. But she discarded that idea. The deranged old men in both countries and good ol' Maggie set up the machine that was about to kill them all. Petrov wouldn't want to hear that... Same with God Save the Queen.

Elvis? Too happy. The Pistols? Too British. Frobisher's Sextet, maybe? Close, but too sad.

She found her answer on the next album. *Of course.*

Persephone pulled the record out of the sleeve and set it in place. A few clicks later and the needletip graced plastic. Pytor Illych Tchaikovsky's 1812 Symphony softly tumbled out of the speakers.

Who better than a gay Russian composer fond of adding cannons to his pieces to see them all out of this world? She sat back down and grabbed the mic off of its cradle. *Godspeed, Simon Petrov and your men. Hopefully the next go round will be better. For all of us.*

She took a sip of tea and clicked the receiver on.

"This is NMF New York to all Motherfuckers. Jackboot, Jackboot. Jackboot. The Tower—upright; Eight Swords—reversed; Queen of Pentacles—upright. This message repeats."

She said it three more times each on seven different channels before leaning back in her chair. She exhaled, the minimum plan complete, the code clear to anyone in the know. Someone will get out.

Maybe I could make it?

She could just leave now, her work was done. She checked the watch, twenty-eight minutes left.

Fuck it. What's done is done. Can't stop the signal. She shook herself, sipped the last of her tea, and took up the mic once more. The crescendo was just beginning when the words that Simon Petrov gave the world left her lips.

"To anyone receiving this message, this is Persephone Tough. I'm a ham radio operator out of New York. Fifteen minutes ago, I received a message from a Soviet colonel who was transmitting over multiple frequencies first in Russian then in English. He claimed their automated nuclear launch system had been triggered and their missiles were being fueled.

There was gunfire in the background and he gave detailed information on the type and strength of the weapons that will be sent our way. I am choosing to believe he risked his life to warn us. If that is correct, the first missiles will be in the air in twenty-five minutes..."

It was 7:07 a.m. New York time.

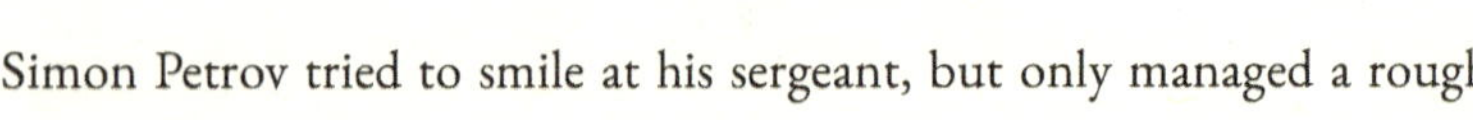

Simon Petrov tried to smile at his sergeant, but only managed a rough twitch of the lips.

"It has been an honor, Gennady."

His thoughts turned to Raisa. She'd be getting home soon. A part of him wanted to laugh. Even now, at the end of the world, he wasn't worried about her. If there was any woman who could survive the coming hours, it was Raisa Petrova.

He wanted to laugh because instead of worrying about his wife's safety, he worried more about what she would think of him. He wouldn't be there for the end, not like he promised when they married. She'd never know why, so would she hate him? Or would she think he remained at his post like a good soldier?

"Simon?"

Gennady's voice was quiet but prodding. That last thought gave him the answer he needed.

"Yes, Gennady, I'm sorry. Everyone, listen up! I do not wish to keep our spetsnaz friends waiting any longer, nor do I want to wait for a slow death to take us all. Give me a weapon and unlock the door."

He ignored Gennady's incredulous stare and looked over his men, his boys, each one of them grim and sad and confused. Simon forced himself to smile.

Of course it would end this way.

"On your feet, all of you! No more tears, no more sadness. There will be time for that later. Now you must be the brave boys I know you can be. Master Sergeant Shukov?"

"Yes, Comrade Colonel?"

"There is nothing more we can do here, but I have one final order for you. Take the men and get them out of here, take the tunnels, shoot anyone that gets in your way and run. Find your loved ones if you can, but tell anyone you can and get them to safety. You will have at least two hours more than our brothers and sisters in the West, so use that time to save as many as possible. I know that you are all men of the highest caliber and it has been a privilege to serve with you. In my eyes, you are all Heroes of the Soviet Union, but the motherland does not deserve you." He thought for a moment, before laughing. "Instead, I name you Heroes of Kronstadt, for we carry their legacy. We shall succeed where they failed and deliver this nation from the tyranny of the fools that are choking the life from this world."

"Comrade Colonel?" Yaroslav's voice was barely audible.

"Yes, my son?"

"What are you going to do?"

"I... I am staying." He straightened his uniform, before looking the boy in the eye with what he hoped was conviction. "I will cover your escape and keep those bastards from following you. You were all conscripted, rabbits forced in a cage. I am the only one who chose to be here and I am an old man. You have far more to lose than I, so I will keep you safe. If anyone asks, tell them you deserted the mad colonel, the traitor to the motherland, who led you astray. Do not speak of what we have truly done to anyone, or you will share in my guilt. Blame me for everything. Do not try to defend me, or they will shoot you. Understand?"

The boy nodded; they all did.

"Alright. Sergeant, get your men moving."

"Yes, comrade commander. Private Konstantin! Front and centre now!"

A thin, reedy looking man stepped forward. Shukov made a big show of inspecting him before looking him in the eye.

"Comrade Private? Are you prepared to serve the people of the Union of Soviet Socialist Republics to the best of your ability? To safeguard them during this time of crisis, even at the cost of your own life?"

Petrov narrowed his eyes at his friend. "What are you doing, Gennady?

Both men ignored him.

"Yes, Master Sergeant!" Konstantin barked, a wry smile on his face.

"Then congratulations on your promotion, Master Sergeant Konstantin. Did you understand the Colonel's orders?"

"Yes, Comrade Master Sergeant. I understood perfectly."

"Very well, carry them out, Comrade. Leave a few grenades for us, if you please."

"Yes, Comrade Master Sergeant."

Petrov stared at him as the sergeant pushed a desk up against the wall. Gennady began stacking rifle magazines on it before he finally met Petrov's questioning gaze.

"I have delegated, Comrade Colonel." He shrugged. "Your orders only specified the conscripted men, and everyone knows that you don't get to be a *starshina* unless you enlist. Besides, will it not be easier to create a distraction with four hands than two? And maybe, just maybe, I can help you get out of here. Raisa will be worried."

He thought about punching the man, knocking him unconscious and ordering the men to take him away from here. It was stupid of him to stay. He had Anya, his own child. Why would he stay here?

Of course... the same reason I *am.*

Then he heard muttering amongst the men, but no footsteps. Konstantin was speaking stiffly to another man, Kravchenko, going through the same pantomime as Shukov. Then it repeated again and again. Quietly, quickly, through each of them, each one promoting the other then passing on the responsibility. Even the Istchenkos.

Miroslav walked up and saluted him, his other hand holding Konstantin's.

"Comrade Colonel, I am happy to inform you that your orders have been carried out." His voice cracked as he spoke.

"Oh really, False-Master Sergeant Istchenko?" Petrov scoffed. "Do explain, and with haste if you please, because I see twenty-three men who should not be here."

"We have ensured there are no longer any conscripted men on the base." His brother snickered behind him. "They must have all deserted. May the Force be with them."

Petrov shot a venomous glare at Shukov, who whistled a tune, pretending not to notice. *You are a bad influence, Gennady. But then again... so am I.*

He shook his head and cocked his rifle.

"Very well... Heroes! Let us go meet our fate and charge into the teeth of hell itself." He rested his hand on the bank-vault-style lock, but then a thought occurred. "Gennady! Do you have any music for us to listen to? I wish to go out in style. Something appropriate to the situation, if you please."

Shukov positively beamed with delight.

"I have the perfect thing... one moment."

He bolted over to the command console and fiddled with the tape player, throwing the contents at the corner of the room before pulling out a new reel from his pocket. A moment later, he cackled like a child before pressing the play button. The entire base's speakers sprang to life, Gennady's black market treasure putting out nothing but scratchy pops and skips for the first little while.

Petrov waited for the static to clear.

And then the cacophony hit his ears. An ill-tuned electric guitar shrieked for several moments, accompanied by drumming played at a such a speed only achievable by someone suffering a full body seizure. An Anglo-Saksii voice followed soon after, but his accent was so thick, Petrov couldn't understand a word.

At the very least, the men, especially the Istchenkos and Konstantin, looked happy. That's all that mattered.

He had to know something, however.

"Shukov?" he shouted over the din.

"Yes, comrade?"

"What is this music?" He glanced slowly at Gennady.

The man grinned idiotically at him.

"Sex Pistols, comrade! Anarchy in the UK. Andropov will finally have his coronary when they tell him. Maybe the rest of the Politburo will go with him."

It was 3:13 p.m. Moscow Standard Time. The missiles began lifting off, just as the chorus started. The brave twenty-four men of AvtoKom Bunker, number two, made their escape, pitting their hope against the forces of oppression arrayed against them.

The Lord of All Gods spoke once again.

Man did stop once again, and remembered their sins and their trespasses and all the violations committed against the Lord of All Gods. They remembered that the Dragon, though bound to their Lord, had first been made by human hands. And it was only then that all the sons of Man also remembered the Name of their Lord.

They remembered that His Name was Oblivion.

They looked upon Oblivion's Dragon and saw him in his terrible glory. Upon his scales were carved thirty and twenty and eight thousand minor sins that they had borne unto their children. Etched into his teeth, the twenty and three hundred and thirteen mortal sins Man committed against each other. They saw his nails and beheld the last thirty and two cardinal sins, those committed against all their myriad gods.

Oblivion spoke and commanded the Great Dragon to bring unto Man His final end. And the Dragon obeyed.

In a single instant, the bustling cities and the temples and the manor houses simply fell silent; their owners and lords and false profits swept away in the hot breath of death; soldiers and the butchers and the mad fell where they stood, their vestments so tainted it could never be worn again. The generals and the admirals and captains surveyed their devastated forces, turned their gaze to one another, and raised their swords. Their austere command obeyed by none but themselves, they made a funeral pyre of the Great Nations of Man.

The Days of Frost ended by the Great Fire that burned for one hundred years.

Those that yet lived through this tribulation were not spared by any design. The minor vassals of the Great Demons, now freed, gazed upon the ruins beheld their Father. The lands of the south, little more than larders and minor pieces in the Long Games of the Frost heard the screams of pain and of madness and beheld their Father. All the remaining fool-lords, masterless warriors, liars, truthsayers, oppressors, slaves, all the surviving children of Men beheld their true and only Father.

They saw the face of their Father, and his Great Work, and knew to not venture forth to the North or the East or the West. They saw the dead and the not-dead and the corpses of the Great Nations and only then the final words of Oblivion came unto them.

"Tempt not the Lord of All Gods, the One Above All, lest he break his rod upon thee once again."

And they listened.

The Ostanni Dni Exegesis; Apocryphus III of Gaichur; circa 275 Anno as-Sirat

RITE OF PASSAGE

BY I J F DYMOCK

Before you stands a man of pride, a warrior that holds his place among ranks of great men. His face is scarred with the fruits of battle, carefully crafted lines forged in the fires of war. Proof that his mettle is strong. He gazes both at and through you, sizing you up into the depths of your soul; the pressure is enormous, overwhelming. He judges your stance, the way you hold your sword. You can only hope that he sees you the way you want to be seen, not the way most see you. If you miss a step, all that is needed to put you back in place is a sharp gaze and a flick of his head. This man before you needs no words as he is a stalwart, a paragon, and a master.

You can see from the way his armour is battered and dented that he trusts the metal coils that wrap around his body. You have heard talk of his mighty blades, both their names mentioned with reverence and respect as if they themselves are warriors of great import and merit: Gangrel and Phoenix. This man, this exemplar of strength and glory, has earned the trust of a nation not his own through his virtue and deeds.

Thoughts come into your mind of things you could say. Admiration, awed mumblings, questions of his origins and experiences, and salutes. That stories of him made you realize something essential about who *you* are, and led you down this path. Nothing seems adequate, however, and you remain frozen within a training routine under the guiding sight of this mighty Hero.

Time passes unperturbed until this point, a moment where you catch yourself becoming too lost in thought. In a concentration-shattering instant you try to catch yourself, but lose your footing. Your stance is broken, and your training abruptly halts as you try to recover from your confusion. Focus gone, you can hear words of disdain as the world returns to your ears, those who observe you notice your mistakes and perceived shortcomings.

Your mind sinks. our superiors know that you missed steps vital to success. Steps you should have known from the first day, that others had been taught from childhood. You figure that you might as well prepare for slop duty, to give up. You will never be as good as your fellow soldiers, hindered by daydreams and "frailties" of a "lesser body." Not that you *wanted* this body. You just want to be like them.

You are about to resign your defeat, but something halts you mid-step. You can feel it on your back. It is not heavy, it does not pierce you as daggers would. Turning your head you meet the gaze of the Hero looking down at you.

His gaze is not demanding, or strict as you would expect from a hardened trainer. His eyes are not judging, like those who observe the trainees—and especially you. They are hard, but encouraging. Harsh, but soft. You don't know how to explain the connection that you feel in them. Your mind reels, but your body straightens.

Pride which had left your body not moments before returns. You can't let the doubters and naysayers win. They will not be victorious today. You did not come here from your small coastal village to be laughed at and thrown out. You did not trek across the country to this nation's capitol, the centre of military training, to become a failure and a spectacle. You did not face hatred for nothing.

No. You came to become a Hero like the one that stands before you now. You came to learn how to fight and protect those who could not do it themselves. You pick yourself up without a word. So what if your body is weaker? So what if they see you as a woman? Even if you *were* a woman, it wouldn't stop you from doing this. You strive to be strong, and to protect. Turning away from the dismayed onlookers, you resume your training.

From the corner of your eye you can see him. The Hero. For a moment, between strides and stances, you could swear you saw him nod and smile. At you.

Welcome to Hel

By Riley Klay Ridgway

October 6, 2091

Ten.

Nine.

Eight.

Seven.

Six.

Five.

Four.

Three.

Two.

One.

Blast-off!

I wished I had a window to look out of. If nothing else, I wanted to wave goodbye to my homeland, watch the Free and Independent Democracy of Alberta, FIDA, get smaller and smaller as it ejected me into space. I looked around at the hundreds of women with me. None of us were expecting to make it back to Earth alive, least of all me. I was too old for this, but I left very little behind. I couldn't feel sorry for myself. No, it was the others I worried about: the mothers who had been deemed unfit to parent and had left their children behind; the teachers, scientists, doctors: ones in the middle of their careers; the trans men who had been separated from their lovers and their hormones.

I cursed FIDA, cursed the NeoTrump Freedom Party. The NFP had come into power not yet three years ago and done so much damage already. Then softly, I entered a deep sleep where I'd stay for the journey across light years and through a wormhole to our new home on Hydrotopic Extraterrestrial Life-sustainer. HEL.

Groggy and stiff, I came to. I wiggled my fingers, then my toes. I'd read about HEL, every detail I could until I was detained in the isolation centre. The mass was just above that of Earth's, the air, breathable... they hoped.

Martin stood. "I know I'm one of the only men here, and I am not trying to reinstate the patriarchy, but we've got to make a plan and come together."

There were a thousand on board. Lesbians, mostly, who the NFP deemed dangerous, blamed for the economic crisis. Nonbinary people and trans men, seen as equally dangerous and who mustn't be shipped off with the gay men. They wanted reproduction impossible.

I stretched my neck and undid my harness. We were here. Wherever *here* was.

There were a couple meals each on the ship, solar panels, and a water filter. After that we were supposed to figure everything out, or die. The government was hoping we'd die. Live long enough to be a science experiment, pave the way for colonizers and then die off, slowly, one by one. Our worthless bodies scattering this planet.

"Martin's right." Uki's copper complexion and black curls contrasted with Martin's fair features and golden beard. They stood next to each other at the lowest part of the spacecraft. The seats were arranged in concentric circles, ten layers up with an opening in the middle that allowed their voices to carry. Uki continued, "We'll need a small team to check out the surroundings, and one person on each floor to report on the health of those with them."

"I'll go out," I volunteered.

"Are you sure?" Uki asked.

At seventy-one, I was the oldest in the group, but it was my age that made me willing to sacrifice. I'd lived a full life. Others couldn't say the same.

I stood and asked, "Who's coming with me?"

Four others were chosen.

Five volunteers stepped into the airlock and hoped for the best. I took the hand of a young brunette woman. I could see fear in her dark eyes.

"I'm Hazel," I introduced myself.

"Maeve," she offered.

I squeezed her hand. Dedicated myself to protecting her.

Two other women, Zayn and Amira, whispered to each other before exchanging a quick peck.

The fifth person, Blake, an enby in their forties, stood alone. They ran their fingers through their short red hair and tried to stand tall.

Suddenly, the air was fresh, salty, and the light was bright after the dimly lit and sterile shuttle.

I gulped in the air as Maeve held her breath. "Breathe," I instructed, "breathe. This is freedom!"

Freedom was more than we could reasonably expect, but the fresh air was a luxury after years and years of forest fire smoke filling our lungs. Yes, the air was exceptional.

Blake crossed their freckled arms over their flat chest and tried to sound confident, but their voice trembled and came out an octave high. "You two go that way, and you two the other." They deepened their voice. "I'll stay here and keep an eye on you. Keep an eye on me. We have no idea what kinds of dangers are lurking around here."

Still hand in hand, Maeve and I looked around. The ground under and all around the ship was covered in polished potato-sized rocks. Bits of vegetation stuck on the rocks, and Maeve bent down to take a closer look. "I think it's a..." Maeve paused. "I don't know. I'm a plant geneticist, and I don't know."

It was green, a single leaf-like being, thick like a succulent, but stuck to the rock like a slug. We watched it for a time, but it didn't move. Maeve picked up the rock to examine the growth closer. It had no roots, unless they grew into the rock. "Our first specimen." Maeve boasted, clutching it tightly.

In the distance, we saw a brightly coloured forest. We looked at it, and then looked back at each other. It was too far, and yet, our feet propelled us forward. We didn't stop to examine the other growths on rocks though they varied in shape, size and colour.

The closer we got to the forest, the less it looked like a forest. The vegetation, if that's what it was, wasn't leafy. There were branches, or limbs, thick and colourful, swaying as if they were underwater. Maeve watched their movements; a frown grew on her face. "It's not like they're blowing in the wind," she observed. "They're moving independently of each other, like they each have a mind."

I thought back to the year 2065, when Alberta made the official move to agave farming. The President of FIDA tried to celebrate the new national plant. Like the agave plants, the limbs or tentacles of the vegetation started from a central point and spread out reaching just over our head. Unlike agave, each tentacle was round, thick like a pool noodle. Like the growth on the rocks, these beings ranged in colours, but they were darker near the ground, and lighter as they reached to the sky.

"Get back!" Blake yelled from their place near the ship. "Run!" Their voice barely made it to us. But it was so silent on HEL that we caught their urgency. Looking back, we could see them waving frantically.

Maeve and I had been too close to realize that the nearer we got to the forest, the nearer the forest got to us. When we returned, we learned that from Blake's perspective it was clear that whatever was out there was keenly aware of invaders. What had looked like random movements to me looked like heads turning to Blake.

Zayn and Amira had wandered in the other direction to the waterfront. The two women walked back to the ship hand in hand giggling. Back on board, they handed in a sample of the water they'd collected and told of the vast sea with ripples rather than waves.

A few of the scientists on board, Maeve included, got to studying the samples, while the rest of us wondered exactly why there were no windows on this dungeon spaceship.

"We've got to get out of here, set up camp on the rocks," Martin insisted.

"We don't know what's out there," Uki resisted. "The way Maeve explained those tree forms, the way Blake said they were watching them. It can't be safe."

They were both right. The ship was suffocating. It was made for transporting, not housing, a thousand people.

"Let's just blow them up," Martin declared. "We'll get rid of them, and we'll make our home."

"No," I said. By the time I had begun kindergarten, the curriculum no longer included the history of Indigenous peoples, but I'd learned from my mom who'd refused to forget the past. I explained the history of smallpox blankets and residential schools to the others, who listened as if they were kids and this was a fairytale. "We can't be colonisers," I concluded.

"Good news!" Maeve called out, emerging from the small, but advanced lab on the ship. "From the looks of it, whatever these lifeforms on the rocks are, we think they're edible. Anyone brave enough to try?"

"Pick me." I stood.

There was resistance, but I didn't sit down and no one else volunteered.

"Just rub a little on your lips, to start," Maeve suggested.

I obeyed, wary of the eyes on me.

When I didn't itch, or swell up, or die, I licked it off my lips.

"Tastes like," I paused, licked my lips again, "it's a little salty. Tastes a little like soap, lemon, lavender and spinach."

"Well," affirmed Maeve, "You tried it, so you get to name it."

"Slols," I declared quickly. I've always liked palindromes.

"I got some good news!" Margo announced. I was happy that everyone turned away from me. Margo was short and looked barely twenty but had the confidence of a CEO. "I've managed to disconnect our outgoing signals. That means those mofos back on Earth won't get access to any of our research. Let 'em think we're dead."

"If they think we're dead," Maeve looked downcast, "there'll be no rescue."

"We don't need them," Zayn declared, dragging her hand through her tangled, straw-coloured locks. "They destroyed the Earth, I wouldn't want them coming here." She glanced at the airlock and added longingly, "It really is beautiful out there."

"It's still, peaceful and warm," Amira added, placing her arm around Zayn's waist.

"This is our home," Martin remarked, intentionally or unintentionally flexing his sizable muscles, "and I'm sleeping out tonight, so I can lay down and have my own space. Who's with me?"

"I'll come," I exhaled, "but we must remember, we are visitors here, or refugees perhaps. We have to respect the life that was here before us."

Martin grunted a kind of acceptance, and asked again who'd come.

Blake eyed the door. "I know I warned about those things watching them"—they motioned towards Maeve and I—"but I think, if we give them space, we'll be alright."

Uki shook her head. "I don't like this," she muttered. "It's a bad idea. You'll be on your own."

Blake gave Uki a longing look.

In the end, Blake, Amira, Zayn, Maeve and about a hundred others all agreed to head out. We made our way outside. The days and nights were known to be short, eight hours each. Eight hours on the rocky shore seemed manageable to me. I didn't know if I'd be able to sleep, but I stretched out at the base of the ship near Maeve, determined to make the best of the night.

"Have you even seen stars?" I asked Maeve. Between the light pollution and the smoke, it'd been years since I'd been able to find Orion or see Cassiopeia.

"Never," Maeve replied. She let out a sigh "I had a girlfriend in university. She took me to the mountains, to see the stars. It was winter, most of the fires were smouldering, not a lot of smoke around. When we got to this dark place, she'd seen them there before," Maeve shook her head, her long straight hair flowing with the movement. "It was cloudy."

"Look." I pointed up. The sky had darkened and the first stars were beginning to appear.

"Wow," Maeve responded. "Wow."

I looked up for the constellations of my childhood, but they weren't there. There were new patterns.

"See that bright one, with an arch of four stars above it?" I pointed. "If you drew lines from the lower one, up to the ones on top, it'd look like the beings we saw in the forest today, and next to it, see those stars forming a triangle, that's our spaceship, that's us. This is our story of being invited in, of us living together in harmony," I interpreted, "and it teaches us to be united, not one above the other, but equals."

"Yeah," Maeve said in awe, "I see it."

A slight breeze came off the lapping water, but it wasn't cold. Regardless, Maeve moved closer to me, our arms barely touching.

"What'd you leave behind?" I nosed.

"My lab." Maeve shrugged. "It's top secret, but I guess that's meaningless now. We were on the brink of modifying citrus, oranges mostly, to be drought-resistant so they could grow in FIDA. It was government-funded research at the university. My team, the student interns, they were all I had. My family are all NeoTrumpists..."

"Oh, I'm sorry," I interjected.

"...and my girlfriend, the one I had in university, she left a couple years back right after the NFP got in power. She moved to Saskatchewan. We argued about it. She wanted me to go with her. She didn't think we were safe in FIDA. I still saw some hope. I thought I offered value to FIDA. I thought they'd care more about my research than my sexuality, but this government came first for those of us working and studying at the university. I guess my ex was right." Maeve studied the sky, then pointed along the horizon. "Is it getting light?"

For a moment I hoped for auroras, but as I studied the sky, I realized a moon was climbing. It came up, reflecting over the water, and we sat up to take in the moment.

"The water's rising!" Blake shouted.

Maeve looked towards the shore and cursed. "We've gotta get to the forest." She shuddered. But when I looked to the forest, it was gone.

We were on our feet. I looked again at the water. It was coming. I took a step back, but the water was gaining. "Run!" I said, taking Maeve's hand. We ran to where the forest once was before we dared look back.

The water had risen up to people's waists. Many tried to get the attention of those on the ship, but it was of no use. The ship was solid and no amount of banging would alert those inside to the danger.

"The water!" Maeve exclaimed. "Let's go!"

In the light of the moon, we saw in the distance a hill, and on the hill was the forest. "We've got to get there," I declared.

I couldn't run the whole way, but we made our way to the hill as quickly as we could. The water was at our heels as we began to climb.

"They're here because it's safe," Maeve observed, motioning at the forest.

When we reached the beings, I didn't dare touch them. I didn't want to get close, but Maeve was right. They were gathered on the highest point, and the water was still rising.

"I'll watch the pl...animals," Maeve said, inadvertently coining a word, "and you keep an eye on the water."

The water was still rising, halfway up the hill. Then I extended my gaze and gasped, "Maeve, look!"

The spaceship, glistening in the moonlight, lifted and tipped into the water. It floated on its side. I thought I could see some heads bobbing in the water that sloshed around it, but feared that survivors would be few. *We should have told Zayn and Amira to run with us,* I thought, wondering if they were still swimming or if they were gone. *We should have told them all.*

"Did no one studying this planet care to look at the tides?" Maeve, indignant at the oversight, cursed loudly.

At the sound, the planimals turned. Their appendages stilled as if listening. I heard Maeve curse again, but this time under her breath.

We were still then, silent. The water seemed to have stopped rising a foot from the top of the hill. I lowered my body to the ground to sit. I watched a rock that was just out of the water. Slowly, it too was submerged so I chose another landmark rock. I took my eyes off of it to analyse the situation with the ship. It rocked back and forth, and if I squinted I thought I could make out some people clinging to its shell. When I looked back for my landmark rock, I couldn't find it. Either the water had risen higher or my mind was tired like my body. I chose a new rock, this time determined not to lose focus, while I took stock of my body. My legs were tired. I hadn't run in thirty years. The rocks were smooth, but my bum wasn't comfortable and my back was beginning to ache. I sighed as I watched the rock go under.

I turned to Maeve. Her eyes were fixed on the planimals, but they seemed at ease, their appendages no longer still and listening. I rubbed Maeve's shoulder and whispered, "The water has slowed, but it's still rising."

"We'll be safe," Maeve assured me, taking hold of my hand. "The planimals are here, they know."

"I suppose," I agreed as I stood and stretched. I couldn't argue because I had no better idea. The hill plateaued on the top and was highly packed with the planimals. There was nothing to do but watch the water slowly creep up to our shoes.

I thought about commenting on the weather. At least it's warm, and we had some flat ground beneath our feet. We had a place to stand. But it all felt meaningless as I looked down on the ship floating away, and the forest blocking us. Maeve and I were truly alone.

We stood through the night. Fatigue wore on me. My feet were wet, but slowly the water began to subside. As soon as the ground below me was water-free, I didn't mind that it was still damp, I lay down on the rocks and stretched out. I didn't have any energy to give to the planimals, not even a thought for our crew mates or Maeve. I was asleep in moments.

Something was tapping me. An elephant vying for my attention, its trunk firm but gentle nudging me out of sleep. When I drifted awake, it wasn't an elephant standing over me but a planimal with a purple pool-noodle appendage prodding my side.

"I think they want us to move," Maeve whispered. I blinked into the sun. Reality was the strangest dream.

The planimals were spreading out. Their root-like bottoms slid across the rocks, inching down the hill. Maeve helped me stand, and we crept along with the others. They no longer poked at us once we were moving.

I tried to scan the horizon, but the planimals surrounded us, blocking our view. "Our crew?" I asked Maeve.

"I don't know," she mumbled.

"If we stay at the top, maybe we'll get a view."

Maeve motioned around. "I don't know if we have a choice."

We were surrounded by planimals all crawling down the hill towards the sea, so we went along with them.

Eventually the planimals spread out and sunk their roots into the rocks. Besides the waving of appendages, HEL was still, silent.

"What do we do?" I asked Maeve.

"I'm exhausted," she admitted. "I say we nap here, and then see if we can get back up the hill and look for others."

"You sleep. I'll keep watch," I assured her. She curled up with her head on my lap. Her soft skin was tan, like the hoodoos of Drumheller. I stretched out too. It was more comfortable than sitting, and pretty soon we were both asleep.

The sun was right overhead when we woke up. Without speaking, we crept to the edge of the forest, back the way we came. Once out of the forest, we snacked on slols, debating how to best describe their flavour, and tried to determine if the different colours had different tastes. The higher we got, the fewer there were.

Our view from on top of the hill was unobstructed. We could see the sea, extending forever in one direction, but behind us lay low hills, some lower—but many higher from where we stood. Then, near the water's edge, we spotted our spaceship laying on its side.

"Let's go!" I squealed.

When we got to it the door was open, some people were hanging out on the rocks nearby, washing themselves trepidatiously in the sea, drying in the sun.

"Hey!" one called out to us. "You're alive."

"We are." I waved back.

"You're the ones who discovered slols," she observed.

I nodded.

She scraped one off a rock with her teeth. "They taste like soggy chips."

"Nah," countered the woman next to her as they wrapped their arms around each other, "savoury gushers."

We laughed and waved as we went by.

Once inside, Maeve headed to the lab. She told me that she wanted to write down her observations about the planimals and throw ideas around with people whose minds worked like hers.

The rest of the women looked like lost children, or better yet, like children on their first day of childcare. Almost in tears, stunned, stuck in place, in need of guidance, comfort, and love. I knew how to engage children with a game, a song or a toy. I hadn't a clue what to do with such a large group of mopey adults. I inquired about the previous night and learned that Martin, Blake and a handful of others had survived. The sea had taken the rest, including Zayn and Amira. I hadn't known them well, but I stood for a moment to remember their affection for each other, to thank them for their willingness to venture out.

Next, I needed to find Martin. He seemed to know how to get a group on board with him. I asked around and was told that he hadn't come out of the bathroom since being rescued in the morning.

There were only two washrooms on board, each with five stalls. When I knocked on a stall and heard a deep grunt, I knew it was him.

"Martin?"

Another grunt.

"I'm coming in," I warned. The door was locked and the whole bathroom was flipped sideways, so I pressed against what had been the floor and crawled in. That was much easier when I was a kid.

"I fucked up," he whined. His broad shoulders slouched.

"Martin," I began, trying to find reason, trying to find space for my body inside the stall. I crouched awkwardly on the stall wall.

"People trusted me. They put their hope in me. They followed me." He clenched his fists.

"You didn't know," I countered.

"I should've known. I should've gone alone." He squeezed his eyes tight, as if he were afraid tears might escape. "I should've found out first. I should've died."

"No one should've died," I opposed. "It's not your fault."

"What if it's just the patriarchy?" He tugged on his beard, as if trying to pull it out. "What if I just think I know better because I'm the man here? What if that's why I thought I had a brilliant idea?"

"Well, was it?" I challenged.

"I did think it would be a good idea. I mean, we can't stay cooped up in this tiny ship for long, or we'll start killing each other." Martin glanced to the floor. "I just didn't think anyone would die outside."

"I'd been out. It seemed safe enough that I was willing to spend the night. All of us who'd gone out during the day, went out again at night."

"When the water started to rise, we couldn't get back inside. We kept knocking, but they couldn't hear us. They had no idea we were in danger until the ship started floating." Martin closed his eyes as if reliving the moment. "By then it was too late."

"Look Martin, the tide is going to come in again. We need to think of a plan. We need to get people organized."

"Not me. I can't be responsible for any more deaths."

"We were sent here to die." I paused, watching him take in the words. "It's FIDA's fault, the NFP. Blame them all you want, but don't blame yourself. They didn't send us to HEL to live."

"I'm not just going to lie down and let them walk all over me."

"I know. You're a fighter. We all are or we'd left FIDA years ago. So, we go out there and make the most of this situation."

"Fuck'em." Martin punched the carbon fibre wall and cursed again, shaking his hand. "What do we gotta do to survive, to thrive?"

I explained my idea and he shook his head. "You're going to need Uki if you want people to get behind this idea. No one will trust me."

I considered his stance, but I didn't think people had given up on him like he thought. "I'll get Uki," I conceded, "and then I'll come back and the two of you will work together to organize this."

I opened the door, hopped out of the stall and headed to find Uki before Martin could protest.

It took a while to get buy-in from Uki and Martin, and then a bit for them to get everyone committed to the work. Then suddenly, we were a team. Uki flung off her shirt and the crowd followed. Shirts were flying off, being knotted together to make ropes. Maeve kept an eye on the planimals. They were moving slowly to higher ground. It meant we had limited time. If we weren't ready, the sea would come and take us away to who knows where.

The ropes were tied to the exterior frame of the ship. Most of us were inside, but Martin led the team of athletic, young folx, ready to tug on the ropes, to direct the ship to higher ground as the water lifted its weight. I'd pointed out the hill to Martin. Not the one where I'd spent the previous night, that belonged to the planimals, but the one slightly higher beyond it. He insisted that I wait safely inside. I felt the ship rise in the water and closed my eyes. I could only hope this plan worked.

When I felt the ship rocking, I knew it was now or never. The airlock was open and I couldn't help myself. I had to go and watch.

"You got this," I cheered as I joined Uki and a few others who were monitoring the situation.

The water was swirling around their ankles, but they pulled the ship along with grace. As they started up the hill, they were able to get out of the water. The sea stopped rising as quickly, and they merely needed to keep the ropes taut to get the ship in place.

It was dark when Martin and his team reached the top of the hill. The team was pulling, but the ship was still on the side of the hill. They pulled hard, but the water had stopped rising.

"We can't crest the hill!" Martin called.

"We need everyone!" Uki replied. "All hands out and helping!"

We poured out of the ship. Many grabbed the ropes while others got behind and pushed.

"We're almost there!" Martin called out. "On three, two, one."

I pulled with all my strength. It wasn't much, but together we got the ship on flat ground. We cheered and then collapsed on the ground. Martin repositioned the ropes and directed everyone back to our feet, telling us where to stand. We heaved on three and got the ship upright. We hugged each other and danced around the craft.

In the morning we surveyed the land. The hill we were on was a vast and wide plateau. High enough to avoid the tide, wide enough to spread out and build housing but there were no slols up there, no vegetation. Many of the women started building homes with the rocks. It wasn't long before Blake found red clay by digging into the ground. It was useful for holding the rocks together and walls were erected. While some focused on housing, others began planting the seeds that'd come from Earth. These were planted both in the small terrarium that had come on the space ship, and in the ground. Crickets and chickens, both from preserved eggs, were hatched and grown in captivity.

In the evening we looked out at the rising sea and remembered those who were no longer with us. We read off the list of all those who'd left the Earth, calling out "present" when our name was said. When no one responded to the name, we repeated it in chorus, once, twice, three times, and then left space to remember, to mourn, to surrender their souls to the sea.

Zayn, Zayn, Zayn...

Amira, Amira, Amira...

Rather than focusing on the plants from Earth, every day Maeve wandered down to observe the planimals. I'd go with her, chatting along the way, but silent as we sat among them. She'd take a notebook, sketch and record her observations. I'd marvel at the place and reflect back on my life. How'd I ever end up lightyears away from the home I knew? How did a place once known for welcoming and accepting all change so dramatically after a little virus called COVID polarized everyone the year I was born? I didn't remember much from those early years when Alberta was still part of Canada. I don't remember much either from the years when Alberta had joined the USA, but whatever had happened, whatever changed Alberta from the place I was born to the place that shipped me away, I didn't want that happening here.

"What about you, what'd you leave behind?" Maeve asked one day as we walked back to home base. It was like she'd had the question forming for a long time, but only now was brave enough to ask.

"Not much," I admitted. "My wife died four years ago. That's when people at work realized I was queer and they forced me into early retirement. I didn't have much purpose left."

"What did you do?" Maeve inquired.

I thought back to the smiles and giggles that'd surrounded me every day. "I was a daycare worker. Three- and four-year-olds. I loved those kids. I never had my own. I never needed my own." My smile shifted to a frown. "Anyhow, once the staff found out I'm queer, they thought I was too dangerous to be with kids."

"I always wanted kids," Maeve reflected. "My ex too, but she didn't want to raise them in FIDA. If I'd listened to her, we might have a family by now, somewhere safe." Maeve sighed. It was neither a happy sigh nor a sad sigh, simply a reflection. "Instead, I've met the planimals."

When we arrived back at base, it was getting dark. Some of the women were coupled off in the shelters they'd made. They wanted privacy, but we could still hear their intimacy. Maeve and I joined a circle of others who were looking up at the stars. Had we had a fire, it would have reminded me of camping with my family when I was small.

"The stars tell stories, you know," I observed to no one in particular.

Eyes turned to me, so I continued. "Not horoscopes, not fate, but lessons to live by." I pointed up at a star.

Look at that bright star," I encouraged. "We have two parallel lines. Not one above the other, but two lines as equals. Once there were two snakes, a green one and a red one. One day, the green one climbed onto a rock, looked down at the red one and declared, 'Look at me. I am above you, I am more worthy than you, so you must listen to me.' The red one scoffed and climbed up onto the rock too. The green one tried to defend its space, but when it realized it couldn't win the fight, it climbed into a tree. Again the green snake proclaimed, 'Look at me. I am the best. Do what I say.' From above, the green snake watched as the red snake built a pole. When the red snake leaned up the pole, it reached all the way to the sun. The red snake started climbing the pole, and the green one raced after it. They got higher and higher until the sun dried them out and they fell to the ground as two sticks, equally humiliated. Years and years passed, the snakes were walked over and kicked about until they were lifted up to the sky, to be a lesson. We know what happens when people start saying that one group has more rights than another. That can never happen here. Let this constellation be a reminder to us, and we'll teach it to those who come after us, that we can never treat one group worse or better than the others."

There was a light round of applause until Uki disputed, "Those who come after us? Who's that—FIDA? Our children?"

"Why not our children?" I challenged. I could practically hear her eyes rolling so I continued. "Humanity has managed to send us here on a spaceship. They modified eggs so we have chickens to breed. Back on Earth we're customizing plants and animals to survive on a dying planet. We have some incredibly smart scientists here, and a decent lab. And you're telling me that we can't make babies without a man? Why not?" I concluded.

Again there was a light round of clapping before groups broke off in chatter. I looked to Maeve, "Do you think it's possible?"

She shrugged. "Sure, I mean, cloning's not a new idea, but I think we could do better than that." She paused as if her mind was scrolling through textbooks, navigating a wealth of information I'd never have access to. "I bet there's a way to get RNA from two women to join in one egg, to make one unique baby."

With time, everyone found a purpose. Some building, others setting up water and sewage systems, and others cooking and preparing food for the group. They found an aquatic sort of soft-bodied worm which turned out to be edible, along with some straw-shaped seaweed. With that, slols, eggs, and crickets, we were getting by, and with the help of a few women who used to be chefs, it tasted much better than it sounded.

Blake was busy extracting parts from the ship, while Uki and Martin sat around envisioning the future.

"I don't think we need a government," Martin speculated, pulling on his beard. "If an issue comes up, we'll all vote on it, like democracy in its purest form.

"But there's a million things that could come up," Uki disagreed. "Are we going to hold a plebiscite every time someone builds too close to their neighbour?"

"We just got to let those small issues go." Martin shrugged.

"But that's exactly it, who's to say what's a small problem?"

"Well not that." Martin pointed at Blake who was coming out of the spaceship with wires and bars that had once played a part inside. "Who's to say they can take from the ship?

Uki pursed her full lips, “Let ’em be.”

“No, really,” Martin stood. “I mean anyone can have as many rocks and slols as they want. I think they’re endless here. But the spaceship is a limited resource. Just ‘cause Blake’s decided to pillage it first, does that mean they can take it all?”

“They’re not taking it all.” Uki got on her feet, matching Martin’s height. She looked into his piercing eyes. “I’m sure they have a plan. I’ll go see what it is, so you can interrupt everyone for a vote.”

Once Uki left to be with Blake, I approached Martin.

“What would you do?” he asked.

I shrugged. “Just remember the snakes.”

I needed a hobby, so I started mapping the stars. When I saw a bright group, a story would come to me and I’d name the constellation. At night, when the moons weren’t too bright, I’d look up and tell a story. Sometimes new ones, “The Chicken and the Egg,” “The Cricket who Flew,” and sometimes the first one I’d ever told, “Unlikely Friends.” Each time I told them, they gained new details and twists. They moved further into fantasy, but never out of reach, never too far away to dream.

On days that I wasn’t with Maeve observing the planimals, or mediating between Uki and Martin as they tried to ascertain the difference between power and leadership, I’d wander into the lab. The scientists were at work studying every new aspect of the planet.

“Maeve won’t let us touch the planimals,” Maha, a biomedical engineer, lamented. She looked into a petri dish observing the microbiome of the sea.

“I think she’s right,” I responded. “I think they’re sentient. I mean how’d you like it if someone took your girlfriend and started experimenting on her?”

Maha had wavy hair, black like Alberta’s oil, and a tanned appearance, but I could still see her blush. “I don’t have a girlfriend,” she stated, looking down to make a note.

I gave her space, and waited for her to say more.

"Not yet." She jittered the petri dish and put it under the microscope. "But I'd like to get to know Maeve more."

"She won't let you take the planimals," I restated, "but you could go with her to observe them one day."

"Do you think..." Maha began, but she didn't seem sure how to complete her thought. She squeezed her hands together and looked over at me with questioning eyes.

"I think she'd be glad for some company closer to her age, rather than hanging out with this old bag of bones." I chuckled at my self-depreciation.

Maha shook her head. "You're not an old bag of bones. You're the heart of us all. You keep us alive, keep us going."

That night Blake surprised us with a song they'd written on a new instrument they'd created by repurposing materials from the ship. They sang it for us once, and then invited all of us to sing along.

"When they shipped us far away
And the ship was all we had
We found a better way
In a far and distant land."

I sang along but out of the corner of my eye watched as Maha approached Maeve. The two smiled and giggled, but I couldn't make out what either of them said. The next morning, I watched as they headed off toward the planimals together.

I joined Uki and Martin. We sat on some of the seats that they pulled out of the spaceship and watched as others went about their work.

"I guess you were right about Blake," Martin admitted. "They took from the ship to benefit the group."

Uki let a grin cross her face. She didn't need to say "told ya so."

"What about you two?" I challenged. "What are you going to do for the good of others?

They scowled at me before looking at each other. "We're figuring out democracy," Martin exhaled.

"No one likes a lazy leader," I remarked. "If I were you, I'd get back in the spaceship, and pull out one of these chairs for everyone. We all deserve a place to sit."

They grumbled as they got up, and got to work. As they brought a chair to each home, they took time to hear the concerns of the others. They heard about the joys and challenges facing each woman, trans man and enby on HEL. As they extracted the seats, they came to share a vision of what society on HEL could look like if everyone had a voice at the table, if everyone had a seat.

I didn't see Maeve or Maha that evening, nor the next day until I wandered into the lab. They had with them something I thought Maeve could never do, the corpse of a planimal.

I was backing out slowly when I caught her eye.

"Hazel," she called. "I-I'll tell you what happened."

I walked back in and looked her in the eye. "Okay," I acquiesced.

"I don't know exactly what happened. We..." She motioned in Maha's direction. "We were sitting in the middle of the planimals, but"—Maeve blushed—"we were looking more at each other than at them. Suddenly, I noticed they were moving, but not like usual. Not away from the rising tide. Actually, towards it. I took Maha by the hand, and we rose, moving alongside them. They all walked to this planimal." She motioned at the life form that was without life, "And it wasn't alive anymore. It was like this, grey and limp. One by one the planimals lifted up an appendage, placed it on this one, and then moved on so the next planimal could do likewise. When it was my turn, I reached down and as I touched the planimal, this sensation took over my body, and I knew, I knew this planimal had more to give. I didn't know how to share my thoughts with the other planimals, so I waited, and when the time came that they moved before high tide, they left this one. We call it Eric." Maeve exchanged a knowing look with Maha. It was an inside joke that I'd never know. "Eric was left behind to be washed away to sea. Maha had the same thought as me, and as we snuck away from the mass, we knew without talking that we had to go back for Eric. When we got there, the rocks had been pushed up against Eric and we had to dig it out and carry it back. Anyhow, we got Eric to the lab, and got to work right away, and we've worked all night on adrenaline and now I'm exhausted."

"Then sleep," I offered.

"Can't," Maeve retorted, "too much to discover here." She directed me to look in a microscope, which I did, but it was meaningless to me.

When I shrugged Maeve said, "I think we're really on to something," and turned back to her work.

The way I tell the story to this generation and the next, when I look up at the sky and see the constellation "Eric's Gift," is of hope after death.

We see Eric lying down, and then growth, the coming of life. I share of Eric, whose death was sad, tragic for the planimals who bid their friend farewell, but Eric's death brought us life. Eric was transported with love and care to our lab, and when the scientists sliced Eric open, Eric opened their minds. The scientists saw marvels they'd never seen before. They had to create new categories to contain the information. Of all the discoveries, the most astounding was about reproduction. Planimals are neither male nor female, nor do they have two sets of parts. But planimals are not asexual either. They mix genes, one with another and another and another. A single planimal can have up to five genetic donors. Us humans, we still just have two, but it was Eric who showed us how with a little bit of science, we could reproduce human life on HEL.

Maeve and Maha weren't the first to have a child. Uki, who'd gotten together with Blake, volunteered to lead the way. With skin the colour of dusty hay bales, big lips and eyes like HEL's sea, the child was truly a mix of genes. She spread hope and joy across HEL. Once it was proven safe and viable, others followed. I even donated my genetic material to a couple of single women who wished to carry. But to all the children, I became grandma, a caregiver while their parents pressed forward to stabilize our village.

The doctor and I were in the rock-walled room with Maeve and Maha as Maeve gave birth to their child. With soft dark hair, and wrinkled fists, they named her Stella.

I loved all the children on HEL, but Stella was extra special to me. With the other children, I squatted down and flapped my arms pretending to be a chicken, or lay on my back and let my arms sway in the air being a planimal, but Stella wanted to hear stories. I told her the stories of the stars, but she wanted more. I told her the stories of Earth, and she wanted to know why. Why had people been so mean? How could people be so cruel? I told her the story of the first days on HEL, of all the knowledge we'd gained since then.

She cuddled against me, closed her bright eyes and mumbled, "Tell me again."

CONTENT WARNINGS

The Tale of the Necrobotanist

Death

Neptune Rising

Allusions to/mentions of sexual activity, swearing, death

Reforged

Transphobia, burns

The Thirsty Armadillo

Dehydration

Tunnel

Spiders, death

Five Clouds, a Little to the Left

Harsh language, violence, nuclear warfare, death, Russia

Rite of Passage

Implied transphobia and sexism

Welcome to HEL

Queerphobia, Trumpism, death

www.ingramcontent.com/pod-product-compliance
Lightning Source LLC
LaVergne TN
LVHW091001080826
845145LV00003B/1076

* 9 7 8 1 7 3 8 2 6 2 0 4 5 *